The Fourth Floor

It was as if Cavan had tr... trap. A deafening tattoo ... brutally into his ears. Light exploded above his head. The room was tilting and coming apart around him. Both the glasses on the cabinet shelf dissolved into splinters. As he swung round, rasping out a howl of terror, his stereo unit was shot apart and the television screen went into a blur of milky fragments.

Then there was an incredible hush, for an interminable, impossible moment.

Standing in the open doorway from the kitchen was a burly man with a squat, crushed head and no visible neck. Behind him were three more who might have been brothers or cousins, all with pump guns. Light from the kitchen splashed out across the ruins of what had once been a living- and dining-space.

'Son, we'd like you to do us a favour.'

JOHN BURKE

The Fourth Floor

Based on the series
created by Ian Kennedy Martin

Thames Methuen

A Thames Methuen Paperback

THE FOURTH FLOOR

First published in Great Britain 1986
by Methuen London Ltd
11 New Fetter Lane, London EC4P 4EE
in association with
Thames Television International Ltd
149 Tottenham Court Road, London W1P 9LL

British Library Cataloguing in Publication Data

Burke, John, *1922–*
 The fourth floor. — (A Thames Methuen
 paperback)
 I. Title
 823′.914[F]   PR6003.U54

 ISBN 0–423–01920–1

Novel copyright © 1986 John Burke

Television scripts copyright © 1986
Outcast Productions Ltd and Euston Films Ltd

Printed and bound in Great Britain
by Richard Clay (The Chaucer Press) Ltd,
Bungay, Suffolk

1 The sun scorched down on the arid scrubland and on the slopes of the Serra de Monchique. Inland it was a hot, parched world with only the olive and fig trees to promise fruitfulness out of the dust. But where the sun spread its warmth above the coast, the harshness was tempered by the blue of the sea and the cool sparkle of summer bungalows in secluded little coves. The smart colonies of German, Scandinavian and British expatriates, remittance men and their bridge-playing wives, formed oases of white walls and red roofs. And there were white sails and gleamingly painted hulls where yachts were moored offshore or in the Vilamoura marina. The dazzle from the sea was echoed in the glistening square on George Payne's yacht, where the surface of his swimming pool was almost as still as the tranquil surrounding waters.

George Payne broke the stillness by splashing to the side, perching on the steps, and thumbing the tiny short-wave radio attached to his swimming trunks.

Two minutes later Alvaro appeared with a silver tray on which stood a tall, chilled glass of white Redondo. Payne took a grateful swig. The sun sought out this wine, too, and struck a blinding flash into his eyes. Years ago he had longed to escape to the sun. Now there was no escaping from it.

It took less than another minute for his mother to come padding along the deck towards the cluster of canvas chairs. She did not sit down.

'You haven't forgotten my hair appointment?'

'No, I haven't forgotten, ma. We needn't leave for another twenty minutes.'

'I hate arriving all flustered at the last minute. And don't call me *ma*. If I've told you once I've told you a hundred times. It's dead common.'

5

'All right, mother, all right.'

'I should think so.'

Mrs Payne creaked down into one of the chairs but looked far from relaxed. She stared at her son, willing him to finish his drink and go and get dressed.

He said: 'Enjoy that last batch of videos?'

'Hmph. Just the same as all the others. Georgie' – she leaned forward petulantly – 'I tell you, I'm getting to feel so shut in here.'

'Shut in? For Christ's sake –'

'And don't swear at me, neither.'

'Mother, your own sun-deck is three times the size of that back yard in Dalston. One walk round the boat and it's more than you ever walked in a month of bloody Sundays back home.'

'So shut in,' she repeated. 'And so lonely.'

He began to get the message, but stalled for as long as possible. 'If you want to invite the old girls aboard for another bridge party, or spend a couple of days with your cronies in Albufeira –'

'Albufairyland. That's what the ex-pats call it.' Mrs Payne sniffed. 'Albufairyland – did you know that?'

'Yes, ma . . . mother . . . I knew it.'

'It'd be nice to see some real old friends again. Just for a change.'

'Like Florrie?'

'What's wrong with Florrie?'

George Payne decided not to risk answering that one. He hauled himself out of the pool, finished his drink, and went off to change. He knew that he would get no peace until he paid for Florrie Hall to fly out to Faro. There would be a gushing reunion and the swapping of old memories, and then within ten days his mother would be fed up with Florrie. It would take George Payne only about ten minutes to get fed up with the old bag.

As they went ashore in the launch, Mrs Payne said: 'A little trip to the sunshine would do Florrie's arthritis a world of good.'

6

He drove her along the main coast road into Albufeira. They were a good five minutes ahead of time, but she was complaining about all this rush and bustle as he ushered her up to the door of the salon.

'You'll want some time to go shopping afterwards?' he suggested.

'I know where *you're* going.'

'See you three hours from now, all right? In the Turial coffee lounge.'

'Remember me to her,' said Mrs Payne grudgingly yet without rancour.

She did not really want to acknowledge Luisa's existence or her place in George's life; but at the same time had no complaints against the girl herself, and had been awkwardly polite to her during the time when all three of them had lived in the same villa – an awkwardness which George Payne had decided to avoid by making different arrangements.

He was finding it a good principle to keep things separate, in different compartments, so you knew how to get at everything when you needed it but did not run the risk of getting them jumbled up and damaging one another. In London he had kept his mother shielded from the realities of his work. She knew the money was coming in, she accepted the new house and all the trimmings without asking questions: her attentive, loving George was a good son, one to be proud of. Inevitably she saw some of his associates from time to time and must have guessed what sort of men they were; she read the papers that one time he had been careless and got into a spot of bother; and things he said on the phone must have told her a lot more. But none of it was ever spoken out loud between them. Only once did she ask him about that grasping bitch in London he had nearly married, and was happy to be fobbed off with an offhand excuse. She was even happier, though again she did not utter a word, when the woman disappeared from the scene.

Mrs Payne was at first content in the luxurious villa her

son rented on their arrival in Portugal, overlooking the golden sands of Praia da Rocha, framed between splendid iron gates and guardian palm trees. When he installed the sloe-eyed, husky-voiced Luisa she had not criticized. But within a very short time he realized that these two elements were not meant to mix, any more than either of them was meant to mix with the property deals in London, which themselves had been kept distinct from what Payne liked to think of as his import–export business in specialized tranquillizers. He was adamant in protecting his womenfolk from the sordid facts of life, and protecting one aspect of his own life from another. A very protective man, in his way, was George Payne: especially when it came to self-protection.

Leaving his mother to the mercies of her hairdresser he drove swiftly out of town to the apartment block above Praia da Oura.

It was not its usual dignified, remote self, distanced from the traffic and shoppers and bars and tourists of the town. Today some huge yellow machine was thunderously carving up a length of road under its very windows, raising a storm of dust which swirled in the air like a million frenziedly dancing midges.

George Payne parked behind the building, as far away as possible from the mess and noise. Once upon a time he would have hung around the workmen for a few minutes, wondering if there was an angle, wondering who might be in there manipulating some useful fiddles. Nowadays he was plumper and less pushy, with a slow smile and a less aggressive chin; and he had come to dislike the idea of dust and grit on clothes such as this sky-blue shirt with toning light grey slacks.

Even indoors the vibration made the building a virtual echo chamber. Not the ideal background for a couple of agreeable, untroubled hours with Luisa.

When he let himself into the apartment the noise hit him again. Sun beating against the glass had made the sitting-

8

room so hot that Luisa had opened the windows, evidently finding the racket preferable to near-suffocation. She had not heard Payne coming. Naked, she was sitting on the couch in a pensive, alluring pose. Her head was bowed over one olive-skinned thigh, while her right hand guided a hypodermic syringe into a shadow of her body which would not be readily visible even to George Payne, who had explored that body many a time and in a variety of different ways.

He stormed into the middle of the room. Luisa let out a shriek, dropped the syringe, and absurdly crossed her arms across her breasts.

He dragged the window shut.

'What the hell d'you think you're doing?' he demanded.

'I did not hear. Not know you are here.' Her English was poor.

'Bloody right you didn't.' He kicked the syringe across the carpet. 'What the hell are you up to? You never told me you were on that stuff. *You.* . . .'

'It is not for long. Not often.' She attempted a defiant spread of her arms. She was exquisite, one of the most desirable women he had ever known.

But he raged on: 'Not for long? Don't you know that once you're on it, it's for keeps? However long that may be. Once you've started, you . . . you. . . . Look, you must be out of your mind, cheating on me like that –'

'I do not cheat, George. Please.'

'Getting yourself hooked like any stupid little slag down Fishermen's Beach.'

'Why you so angry?' Her breasts rose and fell as her own impetuous anger took over from that first breathlessness of fear. 'You never deal, in London, when you were big man?'

'I still *am* the big man, and don't you forget it.'

They stared at each other. Her gaze was the first to fall.

'George, please. It is only that I am alone, so much I am alone.'

9

'Oh, stuff that.' Twice in one day was too much: his mother moaning about her loneliness, and now Luisa. After all he had done for both of them. He wanted to get his hands on somebody, work it out of his system, not just stand here listening to a load of whining. 'Where d'you get the stuff?'

'It is not difficult.'

'I know it's not difficult. Comes up the beaches in every tinpot little sardine boat, every hour on the hour. I want to know where *you* get it.'

'I do not make fool of myself on the beach.'

'Where do you make a fool of yourself, then?'

'Please, George, now we forget it, yes?' Her arms were inviting. Beads of sweat glistened like tiny pearls on her throat. 'Is silly, I know. So I stop, and you forget.'

'When I ask a question,' said Payne, 'I expect an answer. Where – and who?'

'You will not cause trouble?'

'I'll cause a whole lot of trouble. Starting with you, if you don't tell me soon.'

'It is Jaime. The pianist in the bar down the road from Oliviero's.'

'He won't be playing at this time of day. And anyway, I don't suppose you just walk up to him at the piano and he slips the packets out from behind the keyboard. So where do I get to him?'

She shook her head wretchedly. Twice more he asked, and once she said, 'But Jaime is little, is a nobody,' and once she simply shook her head again. Then he hit her. It was the first time he had hit Luisa, but his old skills had not been forgotten. He knew precisely how to make it hurt like hell and at the same time render the victim incapable of crying out or even gasping for at least twenty seconds. It hurt him, too; or angered him, hating her for putting him into the position of having to do this. But there was no way any woman of his was going to get hooked on that stuff. Not without the score being settled.

10

When she could breathe again she told him where Jaime Barreto could be found.

'And you,' he said, 'you stay away from that phone. Stay right where you are. Get it?'

She got it.

In his big-time days in London, George Payne would merely have sent one of his heavies round to deal with the pusher. But out here in Portugal he had been keeping a low profile. So far as anybody knew, he was just another well-to-do ex-pat. If you spread enough foreign currency around, nobody asked questions so long as you didn't force the questions upon them. Start doing business with the local muscle-men, and before long you would be drawn deeper in and the big organizers would start asking what you were up to and just how far you intended to trespass on their territory. Once the Guarda got a sniff of it, they'd be only too happy to join in.

George Payne had taken good care of his income by pulling strings and making people dance in faraway London. Here he had played at being retired. Now, just for this one little matter, he would operate in the old way, on his own. Just like those prehistoric times when he had handled everything personally.

The frontage of the bar, with its discreet restaurant above and a clutter of offices, presented a bland, bleached façade in keeping with its neighbours and similar establishments opposite. The back of the building was less impressive. Dustbins leaked paper rotten with the drippings of discarded carcases, a scattering of broken bottles, and some crumpled cardboard boxes. The rear door had been stained by a thousand greasy fingertips.

Payne opened the door and was confronted by a winding flight of chipped stairs and the button of a lift shaft. He pressed the button, a door squeaked open after an interminable wait, and he was carried up to the fourth floor at a slow, lurching pace. It was not a modern high-speed lift.

It was not actually hauled up by hand-operated ropes, but certainly it would not have caused any financial alarm to shareholders in Waygood, Otis or the like. Not so many years ago there had been a major scandal in Spain over the dangers of hotel lifts with one side missing, giving passengers no protection against the wall of the shaft. After a number of accidents, the Spanish tourist authorities had enforced new regulations on such hotels. The same was true in Portugal – for tourists. Service lifts in blocks used by locals rather than holiday-makers were generally as they had always been. This one was no exception, George Payne noted as he got out, pushed open the door of Jaime Barreto's scruffy little den, and suggested that Jaime might like to come downstairs and have a drink with him.

'*Senhor*, please, I do not understand. I do not know you.' His English was quite fluent, but heavily accented.

'You're sure of that?'

'Perhaps I see you in the bar, sometimes?'

'I don't often drink in joints like that. And I don't care to mix with people who do.'

'Then maybe it is in the club down by the –'

'We haven't met,' said Payne definitively.

'Then I do not know why we meet now.'

'I've been told you supply some dream powders.'

The young man's eyes narrowed. He moved his hands in a gesture of repudiation, then seemed to turn them over as if begging for alms. 'Who tell you this? You are looking' – he was very wary, but ready to be convinced – 'for a supply?'

Payne let him wait for a few moments, then said: 'I don't like drug pushers. Not small-time drug pushers, anyway. And not in my private life.'

Jaime's puffy, complacent features did not so much reshuffle themselves as blend into an impassive pallor. He forced a smile, disclaiming anything that had been said or hinted at before.

12

'Please.' It was a punctuation mark rather than a word. 'Drug? Pusher? I do not understand.'

'You understand too bloody well, little lad. You've perverted a nice lady I happen to know.'

'Do not understand. English – is not very good.'

Payne said: You understand well enough. So listen. I don't like small fry. I don't like you. Before we get too unpleasant about it, I want you to come downstairs.'

'You want to say something, you say it here, yes?'

'No. Downstairs.'

'Do not understand.'

Jaime did not understand until they were in the lift. Then, as Payne's right hand reached for the button, his left hand chopped across Jaime's neck. Jaime went down face forwards, his hands groping out to grip something, anything. As his fingers curled over the rim of the lift floor, Payne's index finger pressed the button. The lift began to descend. This time Jaime screamed. On the slowly ascending wall of the lift shaft was a pulpy smear that had once been an integral part of the pianist's fingers.

Payne stopped at the next floor. 'What a deplorable accident!' He patted Jaime consolingly on the shoulder and stepped over his convulsively twitching body. A howl like that of an animal in a trap – or an animal released, maimed and in agony, from a trap – followed him down the stairs.

The establishment would need a new cocktail bar pianist that evening.

Back at the house he found Luisa still naked, as if she had felt that by staying that way she would lure him back where he belonged, blotting out all the silliness of that mistake. A mistake: wasn't that what it had been, wasn't that all it was?

'All right,' said Payne, 'you can go now.'

'Go? I go where?'

'Anywhere you like.'

All at once her knowing, supple body was gawky and unco-ordinated. Her hands strayed helplessly, without purpose. She could not coax him towards her, thrust him away, do anything but flap about like a clumsy landbound fish.

'Please. . . .'

'And for God's sake don't go on bleating "Please". I've had bellyful of that today.'

She got to her feet. Everything that had been so seductive was sagging and despondent. 'George, I make mistake. I know. Is wrong, is silly. But now you will help.'

'Don't rush it. Take your time packing. But start now.'

'What will I do? I need you.'

'Need me – or the money and the drugs?'

'George, you help me, I will be fine. I promise. Please, you get me what I need, you take care of me, I give you what you need. Yes?'

'No,' said Payne.

By his own standards George Edward Payne was quite a puritan.

A week later a well-fed, well-dressed Dutchman by the name of Yaap de Ruiter stepped out of an airport taxi on the corner of the Avenida Eduardo Rios and strode masterfully into the hotel foyer of the Turial block. His strides thereafter numbered three before two men came out of the Esplandido restaurant and without haste or any particular demonstration of hatred stabbed him eight times. Before anyone else had realized what was happening they walked out into the street, where the same taxi was waiting, and had themselves driven at some speed to the airport – not to Faro, but direct to Lisbon. It was assumed later that they had returned to Amsterdam, having accomplished their mission.

The circumstances of the killing as reported in the local English-language news sheet and on television, and gossiped about in local bars, interested George Payne, from a purely professional point of view anyway. The recent defection of Luisa from the pattern he had prescribed for

14

her added a personal note. Rumours of a drug ring, a battle for control, the elimination of one Dutchman to make room for another, all brought a quickening glow to the embers of Payne's old interests.

The flames really began to flicker upwards with the subsequent murder of three officers of the Guarda Fiscal, the armed Customs Police, on the beach at Olhos de Agua. It must have taken place one night while George Payne and his mother were asleep on the yacht, not more than a mile and a half along the coast. Published stories reported that two of the men had been shot by the gun of the third; but there were conflicting tales about the death of that third one. Rumour had it that the whole thing had been a plant, and that the officers had been killed while intercepting a drugs landing on the beach – or while demanding too high a rake-off from the smugglers.

Either way, it was clumsy. There were dramatic stories of feuds and blunders within the Dutch-run local organization and its headquarters in Amsterdam. Somebody somewhere had bungled. There was a reek of amateurism and incompetence about the whole affair, a hopeless lack of discipline.

George Payne's professional susceptibilities were offended. He had never been able to stand amateurs. Despite his earlier resolutions, the temptation to intervene and put the whole operation on a sound working basis was well-nigh irresistible. Remote control of profitable investments in London was not stimulating enough. He had been on holiday too long: he was getting flaccid. It was time to take some healthy exercise, he decided, no matter how unhealthy that might prove for other people.

The coastal drugs traffic along the stretch from Sagres to the Spanish border was difficult to check, in spite of the resourcefulness and ruthlessness of the Guarda Fiscal. Any shrewd operator with a mind to it could combine fishing with smuggling along that ragged sequence of little bays and coves. There were a thousand difficulties in the way of catching so many part-time dealers, who knew more of the waters and the sands than the most highly trained Guarda. But that also made for similar difficulties from the big-time distributors' point of view. If it was hard to catch drug runners, it was equally hard to coordinate them. The runners came in and out where and when it suited them, and sold to whoever was nearest. The more practised peddlers sometimes worked through a tangled web of bars, souvenir vendors, tobacconists, and even a photographic shop. Sailors offering gold watches and implausible stories to tourists would size them up and decide whether to risk offering hash, heroin and cocaine as well. A few daring loners were known to drive down the Tunnel road, through the dripping arch out on to Fishermen's Beach, and sell their wares in broad daylight. One alarm, and they would be back into the gloom of the tunnel.

There were too many cowboy operators, too many loose ends. George Payne decided to knot them all up together. Without Luisa, he had a lot more time on his hands. He would use it to some satisfying practical purpose.

First he went to call on Jaime Barreto. Jaime tried to close the door in his face. Payne's shoulder was out of practice, but was still strong enough to slam the cringing young man back across the room.

'You do enough.' Jaime held out his crushed and bandaged hands. 'No more. What do you want?'

'Not a lot,' said Payne amiably. 'Look, sonny, let's face it. You're not going to play *Love is the Sweetest Thing* any more. Pity. I'm told you had quite a good style. But where's the money going to come from now?'

'I will live.'

'And I can guess how. So why not let me give you a few tips?'

'You? I want no –'

'I'll make it worth your while. More than you ever got from those wandering cheesemongers. If you play it my way, that is. And from now on there isn't any other way.'

'You will leave, now.'

'For a start, I want the contacts. Not the little ones. I want to know who's supposed to be in charge on this patch.'

Jaime Barreto pretended to have no idea what Payne was talking about. Then he said that it was more than his life was worth to name any names. Then Payne started naming sums of money, and Jaime started naming names.

It was all so simple, when you concentrated. Without his own name coming into it until he was sure of his ground, Payne got Jaime to pass the word along and bring words back, hinting at an international syndicate capable of straightening out all the internal problems of the existing set-up. Let a real organizer get in there with the resources to put the whole floundering lot of them back on the straight and narrow.

He edged his way towards the key men in Amsterdam, Geneva and Paris; then put his own key men to work. Somebody died in odd circumstances in Marseilles, and there was a nasty incident in the Paris Métro, but otherwise very little violence was needed. And still the challenge was not what Payne had wanted: there was no spice to it. All the middlemen concerned were like a lot of small-time clerks, neatly doing as they were told, collecting their payments, and hoping they would live to pensionable age.

All too easy. George Payne sprawled on the deck of his yacht, aware of his mother carefully not asking him why he never went to see Luisa any more, and contemplated the blue infinities of the Atlantic.

It had taken a long time and a hell of a hard slog to get here and buy himself this view. All through the rough years he had promised himself the lot, one day. Now he had it. The lot. He could look at it every hour of his life.

The businesses that supported his way of life went on their way without a sound or smell of them reaching him across the intervening miles. He had picked his men at home carefully and could rely on them. Sometimes recently he had had a few doubts about Monroe getting ideas above his station. But did it matter too much?

Payne edged towards the pool and shed his robe on the hot planking.

In the middle of this warmth, under this glowing sun and radiant sky, he knew that it sure as hell mattered. David Monroe was in the thick of it, getting all the kicks. He, George Payne, was no longer there. Nobody cared much where George Payne was. His tracks had been too well covered for anyone to come looking for him. Everything had worked out exactly as he had meant it to work out. Nothing else mattered in the long term. He was sure of that. He willed himself to be sure.

It mattered.

Before he really and truly retired, Payne hankered for just one spectacular coup: something that would go down in everyone's book of records. He couldn't just let himself fade away in comfort. There had to be something colossal, something that would make the front pages the way Ronnie Biggs and the rest of them had once made the front pages, only this time big enough to eclipse every train robber and bullion thief in the world. And if he got caught, his memoirs would be all over the middle pages, sold to the highest bidder.

Not that he was going to get caught.

It began to take shape in his mind, a daydream so crazy that it had to be grabbed and made real. Just one last fling, to show the energy was still there, the adrenalin could still flow.

Payne slid into his pool and floated on his back. The sun caressed his forehead, but he took no notice. Payne's mind was already busy. He had made his decision. He was going back to London.

2 Rodney Cavan opened the door of his office, glanced along the corridor at the clock, and was content, as ever, with his own intuition. Without even looking at his watch he had known there were just two minutes to go before it was time to leave, and this morning had noted that the wall clock was ten seconds slow. His own watch, a Christmas present from his wife on his own recommendation, had a year's guarantee of not losing more than ten seconds every six months. He checked it every day against the Greenwich pips. Check and double-check, that was his life: every second, every detail just right.

He tidied his desk, tapping one sheaf of documents into a neat pile. It was unthinkable to depart in the evening without squaring things up: he could not bear to arrive in the morning and be faced by papers at odd angles, loose leaves sticking out, a file not put away.

It had been a good day. One of his hunches – though he hated to consider them as anything so random as a hunch – had been proved right. Just a sniff of suspicion and he had known how to pounce and have the man wheeled in. The big chap with his big suitcase and haughty voice had broken out into wild bluster at the end and called him names.

'You snivelling little creep. You and your thick-eared friend here. Think yourselves clever, I suppose? Picking on me and letting the big-time villains waltz through loaded with the stuff. Easier to pick on someone like me, eh?'

'You're not denying, sir, that you have in your possession –'

'Crap, that's what you are. I can smell you from here.'

Cavan had not been offended. He loved it when they cracked up, especially the big, loud ones. He was in a good rosy mood as he got into his Vauxhall Astra and turned towards the quiet seclusion of the lanes beyond Maidenhead.

Monroe had chosen Cavan after the most thorough consideration, though Cavan was not to know that: not for a little while yet. Nor would he have cared to know precisely why Monroe and Monroe's big boss in the background had assessed him as the ideal choice.

George Payne had analysed Monroe's recommendation, and seen where and how to get at Cavan. If he had been a writer of psychological novels he could have drawn the most convincing and vivid portrait of Cavan and predicted his every mood and every move under every kind of circumstance. Payne was not, however, a writer of psychological novels. He was not even a reader of them. He was better and swifter at reading ledgers, ground plans, and the faces of people to work with or smash to a pulp. And Monroe was a gifted disciple with an even more intense preoccupation with figures. Give Monroe a folder of garage worksheets, the ledger of takings and outgoings for a month, and one glimpse of the forecourt, and he could have told you within the nearest fifty quid who was fiddling what and just what the percentage rake-off was. The same went for restaurant owners, diamond dealers, and drug pushers.

Neither Payne nor Monroe was especially interested in statistics of addiction, despair and death, though. Such things came later, after their own books had been made to balance the way Payne wanted them; and who cared what side issues of murder and mayhem resulted from getting that balance right?

Nothing mattered but results. And you got the best results by knowing how to size people up. Payne was good at sizing up those he needed.

Tony Webb, MP, could have vouched for that – if the thought didn't give him the shivers and reduce him to silence every time George Payne's name floated through his memory.

Rodney Cavan was going to become another of that band who learned things they had never thought of signing on for in the first place. Monroe had chosen; Payne had approved: Cavan was the one.

It was dark as the Astra slipped through the thinning traffic and on to the westbound M4. Cavan tapped a cassette into the player, and his feeling of well-being increased as the austere certainties of a Bach chorale filled the car. He pulled off at the turnoff towards Maidenhead, encountered an unexpected rush of cars heading for London, and then neatly slotted into the right lane for his usual route into the more secretive countryside. Without even glancing at the speedometer he could have said exactly how fast he was travelling. Anyone who observed him regularly could have told you precisely when he would slow for the crossroads, precisely when he would slide into the filter as he approached the next lot of traffic lights.

Monroe had in fact observed him regularly. A neat, predictable little man, this Rodney Cavan. Good at his job because his own love of routine made it easier for him to sense when somebody else's routine had got suspiciously out of step. The job, the uniform, the promotion just before his fiftieth birthday, the move from Slough to a nice little detached bungalow with no neighbours to disturb them, no dogs, no distractions, the favourite television programmes at reliable times and the *Daily Telegraph* punctually delivered every morning from the village stores three miles away – this was the pattern Cavan had created for himself and with which he was well pleased.

It was inconceivable that the pattern should ever be broken.

The chorale ended, as he had calculated it would, as he turned up the narrow lane with its windbreak of plane trees. When he had drawn up under the car port he carefully put the cassette away in its case, took up his briefcase, checked that all the car doors were locked even though there was never anybody around here at this time of the evening, and let himself into the hall.

'Dear?'

He said it automatically as he laid the brief-case on the hall chair and headed towards the large open space which the estate agent had assured them was the very latest in contemporary design. It had not originally been to Cavan's taste. He preferred small, well-defined rooms which corresponded to specific functions, rather than this combination of living-room and dining-room with its glass-panelled kitchen divider; but the awareness that he was housed in smart, modern style was beginning to fit itself into his vision of life.

'Sherry?' he asked with a touch of irritation.

Madeleine was usually there ready and waiting, with the tray and the glasses and the decanter which had been a wedding present all those years back in Streatham. He heard a sound in the kitchen, beyond the half-open door, but when he called 'Dear?' again there was no reply. She had not even bothered to switch on the standard lamp, and the light from the shaded table lamp near the fire was feeble by the time it reached the cocktail cabinet. Cavan reached for the sherry decanter with one hand and the switch of the standard lamp with the other.

It was as if he had triggered off a booby-trap. A deafening tattoo of gunfire smashed brutally into his ears. Light exploded above his head. The room was tilting and coming apart around him. Both the glasses on the cabinet shelf dissolved into splinters. As he swung round, rasping out a howl of terror, his stereo unit was shot apart and the television screen went into a blur of milky fragments.

Then there was an incredible hush, for an interminable, impossible moment.

Standing in the open doorway from the kitchen was a burly man with a squat, crushed head and no visible neck. Behind him were three more who might have been his brothers or cousins, all with pump guns. Light from the kitchen splashed out across the ruins of what had once been a living- and dining-space.

'Son, we'd like you to do us a favour.'

The glowering hoodlum stepped slowly out from the doorway, crunching over the débris to switch on a table lamp which, by chance or by calculation, had remained undamaged. As he moved, Cavan saw past him: saw his wife crouching terrified on a kitchen chair, with a gun pointing at her head.

He had to say something. There had to be something to say, shout, scream, yell ... but in nightmares you don't speak, you struggle for words and they stick in your throat and you strangle on them, keep forcing them until a sound works its way through the glue and you wake up and your wife asks whatever you were making that awful noise for.

He gagged, tried to wake himself up. But this was no dream.

He stared at the unbelievable sight of Madeline crumpled up and fighting for breath.

'She'll be fine' – the grating East End voice was almost soothing now – 'if you don't talk to the law. And if we get what we want.'

It was crazy. Cavan shook his head. Inside, it, words were freed at last. 'But what do you want? We haven't got any money.' He looked round at the devastation. 'We haven't got anything.'

'Oh, there's something. Just a little something.' The man stared with implacable, evil good-humour at him.

Yes, Monroe had picked the right team and the right victim. Hanley and his heavies knew how to put the frighteners on anybody. Even their own sort of folk cringed when they saw them coming. A little man like Cavan was easy meat. You didn't have to beat him up, not even the tiniest little bit. No need to mess up Cavan and his wife. Just mess up their tidy little home, smash their things up before their very eyes, and let them draw their own conclusions. *This time it's the telly. Next time it could be you.* The telly:

they were so used to watching violence on the telly, enjoying it from the comfort of ther own armchairs with a glass of sherry or cup of drinking chocolate to hand, so used to guns and fists and villains coming out of the screen at them that they had been pretty well warmed up for the real thing when it hit them. Only it hadn't hit either of them physically. Probably there would never be the need. A little bit of emphasis, that was how you made your point. It saved having to do things twice over. Never try the soft approach first: let all hell loose, and then switch to the reasonable line, always with the memory of that hell blazing in the background.

'I can't think what you want,' Cavan sobbed.

'I'll tell you what we want.'

Hanley jerked his head at one of the men near Madeleine Cavan. Denton was smaller than his leader, but had something powerful coiled inside him that could be lethal if the tension snapped. He seemed to enjoy himself trampling splinters of glass into the carpet as he went towards the hall. But when he closed the front door behind him he did so very quietly. Everything now had gone so still.

Hanley kneed a fireside chair towards Cavan, considerately brushing a few slivers of wood off it.

'Make yourself comfortable.'

Cavan tried to shake his head and put up some show of defiance. But his knees were going to betray him. He let himself sag down on to the chair.

Hanley said: 'Listen. And listen carefully while I tell it.'

He told it.

It was growing more incredible, more awful. Now Cavan was shaking his head. 'No, oh no.' It was all so insane. 'No, there's no way I could. . . .' He shook his head and could not stop it shaking.

'You have to find a way,' said Hanley. 'We know you make regular visits, it's part of your job.'

'But I can't wander through top security buildings taking pictures. You've no idea what it's like in there.'

'Oh, but we have. Quite a few ideas. What we want is a lot more detail. Bags of confirmation. You've got access, you're trusted, they're used to you going in and out all the time.'

The enormity of it ought to have been enough to blank Cavan's mind off. Never mind being beaten unconscious by these villains – just what they were asking ought to lay him out. He would have prayed for unconsciousness, but here and now there was nobody to pray to: nobody who was likely to listen.

From outside a faint purring sound announced a car drawing up the drive beside the porch. Denton came back in. This time he did not close the front door but stood just inside it, waiting.

Madeleine Cavan was forced to her feet. She began to collapse. Expressionlessly the two men on either side got their arms under hers and half carried, half dragged her towards the door. Cavan wanted to fling himself in the way, somehow stop it going any further. There had to be a stop, had to.

But he could not even get to his feet again. As his wife was heaved through the doorway towards a waiting Mercedes, he put out a hand helplessly.

'It can't be done. I'm telling you it can't be done, I'd never get away with it. I swear –'

'Just swear that you don't intend bringing the law round here. Or anywhere round that office or warehouse. And I'm telling *you* that it's *got* to be done. Right? Then when we're all happy, you get the little lady back.'

Cavan mouthed a plea, but his voice had betrayed him again. Hanley was not even bothering to wait. At the door he looked back and said: 'Just do as you're told. And quickly. We'll be in touch.'

They were gone. Cavan got up at last, swaying in the middle of the ruins, the desecration of everything he had built up over the years.

There was no way he could do what they asked. But if

he didn't ... Madeleine ... they hadn't said what they would do to her, and when it came to it they wouldn't really do anything. He tried telling himself that, tried shutting out the reality of those men's faces. It was all a bluff, the only thing was to sit tight and say there was nothing doing, he couldn't do a thing for them.

They wouldn't harm Madeleine. It would do them no good, where would the sense of it be? Sit tight, and she'd be returned.

He looked round at the shambles.

George Payne, miles away, knew: Monroe had done his homework well, and Payne knew that even though Madeleine Cavan was a dreary nagger and that after thirty years of marriage there was nothing of the gallant knight about Rodney Cavan, there was no way Cavan could just shrug her off, leave her to whatever they chose to do to her.

Let him stew for twenty-four hours, telling himself it couldn't be done. Then a pleasant little phone call, and Cavan would play ball.

So that was one key figure nicely fitted into place.

There were several more who suspected as little about their immediate future as Rodney Cavan had done. Everybody was vulnerable somewhere, at some moment in time. All you had to do was calculate where to lean, where to apply pressure. Sometimes it was almost too easy. But, like they said, it was fun finding out. George Payne was beginning to feel the old tingle of pleasure, the buzz you only got by being right in the middle of the action. There was something like a tightening of strings on his fingers as he set the puppets in motion, telephoning Bombay, Geneva, Paris and Amsterdam.

Some of his agents were delighted by an increase in business. The old bastard was back on form, really getting back into the act. Some were alarmed: they preferred to be left to their own devices and not have to account too closely to the inquisitor leaning more and more heavily on their shoulder. And some were puzzled by certain instructions; but then, George Payne had always believed in keeping even his closest associates puzzled for a large part of the time. Nobody must ever know too much: not even his confidant, accountant and trouble-shooter, Monroe. Perhaps Monroe least of all. There was always a danger of Monroe outgrowing his boots.

But for the time being Monroe was in on the action. It was Monroe who sat in the London Embassy Hotel on certain dates, waiting for certain calls from Heathrow; Monroe who took the messages and then relayed them, not from the traceable phone in the hotel but from his car phone, to the police.

It amused both Payne and Monroe to think of those baffled officers in the Serious Crimes Squad sitting there on the fourth floor at New Scotland Yard wondering when the next call would come, and why: frustrating for them, to be fed information which invariably proved accurate, without knowing why they were getting it.

The sequence was nice, neat, unvarying. It might almost have appealed to that poor tidy little creep Cavan, if Cavan were not by now past finding anything appealing.

Arrival at Heathrow of Air France AF 818 from Paris. Ennis on the phone: 'Landed.' And Monroe making his call to the Yard, enjoying the faint rustle in the background.

'Guv, I think it's him.'

A pause, and: 'Chief Inspector Haldane.'

'It's me.' Monroe used the same tone as he had used for the previous calls. They had given up asking what his name was, or what proof he could offer that he was telling the truth: they had by now had plenty of proof.

'Right. Go ahead.'

'Air France AF 818 from Paris. Khalid Khan.'

'Spell that.'

'Oh, come now, chief inspector.' Monroe was enjoying himself. 'They must pay you for something.'

He did not intend to be chatted up for too long. Of course Haldane would be hoping to delay him while they tried to trace the phone. Probably they could identify it as a direct dial car phone from the wave scatter; but out of the thousands in existence they would find difficulty in tracing it to Monroe's Mercedes.

He replaced the phone, and in his head timed the sequence taking place some distance away at Heathrow. It was all routine, all predictable from now on.

Khalid Khan would be waiting for his luggage to come through into the Customs Hall. When he saw his bags he would gravely lug them forward, make a declaration of innocence, and hope within a few minutes to be outside and on his way with nothing declared. Innocent travellers did it every day, by the thousand. And some not so innocent ones. Today there were two Customs officers all ready and waiting, perplexed by the flow of information from the fourth floor at the Yard but prepared to cash in once more. They were, as ever, courteous; but wasted no words.

'Mr Khalid Khan?'

'Yes.' The poor set-up sucker would naturally be alarmed that out of the blue they should somehow know his name and single him out. 'Yes, sir?'

'I wonder if you'd mind coming with us, sir.'

And if he tried to pick up his own suitcases they would politely intervene and carry them for him: all part of the service.

This would be the seventh in a row that Monroe had delivered to the authorities. One aspect of the operation about which he could only guess was the quality of the police guesswork: what the hell were they making of these unsolicited gifts, and what the hell were they aiming to do about it all? It made for entertaining speculation, but it was a pity that more of the picture could not be brought into focus. Ennis reported as much as he could from Heathrow, Hanley could account for every move the hapless Cavan made, and the general pattern could be efficiently assembled. But there was nobody to report accurately on each word and move of the police.

Both Payne and Monroe would have enjoyed watching the exact reactions to their moves rather than having to play in the dark, like a game of chess with all the opponent's tactics masked. But Payne comforted himself with the thought that the police, too, could see only a few pieces at a time and, since the opening gambit had been Payne's, could surely not work out any logical relationship between them.

By the time they reached the endgame and got a glimmering of what those opening moves had been about, it would be far too late.

3 It was a dark night, and a drab one. The two of them sat in the Sierra beside a greasy Limehouse pavement and gazed without any wildly heroic enthusiasm at a house frontage opposite. Its end wall dribbled peelings of old wallpaper and brick dust on to the neighbouring derelict site. The house itself might not be derelict, but it was not what you'd call a desirable residence.

Detective Sergeant Jim Collis unwrapped his third packet of gri-sticks and began to munch.

Detective Sergeant John Miller twitched, as a music lover listening to a magnificent recording might twitch if someone started chopping firewood in the same room.

Collis, spraying a few crumbs over the plastic wrapping and trying to tip them into the ashtray, glanced sideways and said with unnecessary force: 'Right, then. Irish joke.'

Miller stared straight ahead. Of all the things in this world that he least wanted to hear at this minute, Irish jokes took top place. Vanessa's bloody Irish boyfriend was no joke.

'I'm not interested.'

'You will be. It'll slay you.' Collis was bored; and when Collis was bored, he had to keep talking. His brooding face wtih those dark, deep-set eyes was sombre and aggressive, but there was something deeper than that – something defensive, fretting, something that came out as a talkative pushiness to hide his own uncertainties. He had started this joke and he was bloody well going to finish it.

'I mean it,' said Miller tautly. 'I don't want to listen to an Irish joke.'

Collis squashed the gri-stick wrapper in his palm and tried to push it into the already overloaded ashtray. 'Second World War,' he persisted. 'Englishman, American and Irishman captured by Japanese. All about to face a firing squad in a jungle clearing. You with me?'

'I'd rather be without you.'

'Englishman says to Irishman and American, 'We'll each create a diversion, confuse the firing squad, run into the jungle, and escape.' Japanese about to shoot, and the Englishman points behind the firing squad and shouts, "Earthquake!" Japanese turn round, the Englishman belts off into the bushes and escapes.'

'Look, I've told you –'

'Hold it. They line up again, ready to shoot the Yank. He shouts out, "Flash flood!" Baffles 'em – they turn round wondering what the hell – and he's off into the jungle like a dose of salts. So it's time to shoot the Irishman. And what does the Irishman shout out? . . . "Fire!"'

John Miller thought of his daughter, and the bitch who had once been his wife, and the Irishman who was waiting to carry them both off – if he was allowed to get away with it – and he said stonily: 'That isn't an Irish joke. That's *the* Irish joke. The original. Where d'you get your ten-year-old copies of *Beano* and *Dandy*? When are you going to start reading big books without pictures?'

Collis was not even troubling to look at him. Sloughing off his boredom, he was leaning forward an inch or two, taking in a little scene by a terrace of what had once been rather trim little cottages and now were the leftovers of a vanished, swallowed-up world. Two elderly ladies beneath a street lamp were carrying on an earnest conversation: really elderly ladies, not the kind of old slags Miller and Collis were detailed to be surveillancing. One old dear was pointing to her hip, and then to her foot. Her friend was nodding gravely, and obviously preparing to take over with a recital of her own symptoms.

'What d'you think that is?' asked Collis.

Miller studied the weird miming and hazarded a guess: 'The Lambeth Walk?'

'Nothing free and easy about that.'

'Hip replacement, maybe.'

'She's pointing down. It's her knee. Or varicose.'

'Her foot?'

'Fallen arches?'

The old lady, determined not to let her friend interrupt, seemed to be on the brink of falling over as she managed in one complicated contortion to point at her hip, knee, and shin.

'Hip, knee *and* varicose,' said Miller. 'Looks like the full hundred-thousand-mile service.'

It was the sort of irrelevance you needed to keep you going. Or keep you staying. Hours of surveillance when there was damn-all to survey. Dingy streets, hours of hanging about, longing for entertainment. It came to something, thought Miller glumly, when the possible ailments of two geriatrics were the best floor show you could hope for.

Collis suddenly wiped his hand across the thick black hair that hugged his forehead like a roll-over garage door, ready at a minute's notice to slip down over his eyes. He half turned towards Miller.

'Look, I just thought. Sorry. I mean, that Irish joke. I'd forgotten. I didn't mean to –'

'Forget it.'

'How's it going? Any news?'

'You'll be the last to know.'

They slumped back in their seats. The old dears mooched round a corner and were gone.

John Miller's father had been a Met policeman, his mother a schoolmistress. They had not exactly pushed him into being good at school and then continuing to climb, but the whole atmosphere at home had told him what was expected of him. Steady application was a way of life. There were books in the house, and reading what stood on those shelves was what you did with your spare time. Spare time was what was left after doing homework, even when no homework had specifically been set at school. His minor public school held no disciplinary terrors for him: he was well trained for any challenge. He had an IQ of 153, but had learned to keep quiet about this, especially when he followed his father into the Force.

It was not too difficult to keep quiet. He rose to become sergeant at an earlier age than ever happened in his father's day; but then, things had to be faster and tougher today than they had been then. The image of the police changed every decade, and the current one was hard and savage and nothing to do with neighbourly bobbies on the beat. Yet he remained self-effacing in a way which baffled a lot of his colleagues and some of his superiors, keeping his brightness under wraps and using it according to his own instincts rather than the book of rules. Those superiors knew he was good, otherwise he would not have been promoted that speedily. But he could make them feel uneasy when it suited him: he knew when they were unsure of their footing, knew which of them talked off the tops of their heads, and could keep them in suspense while he demonstrated the better things that could be produced from inside the head rather than off the top. His public school, minor as it might have been, had added to his cool confidence: he had the knack of making people listen to him and, even when they resented it, do what he said. It proved very useful.

It had proved less useful in his private life. That was a mess. One of the people who had grown out of listening to anything he tried to say was his wife. The woman who *had been* his wife. This was something he had still not learned to face up to: he still could not quite believe that it was now all in the past tense.

Sometimes he envied Jim Collis. Collis was forever moaning about his entanglements with women, yet somehow there was always a way of wriggling out of those entanglements without getting hurt. For all his exaggerated miseries, Collis got away without too much pain on his own side, and did not seem unduly worried about pain for anyone else. Collis, you could say if you were in a bad, bitchy mood, was dead ignorant and all the happier for it.

Only that was not true. Collis was not ignorant. He had been born in Ealing, had a thickset mongrel determination about him, and had probably come second or third in a lot of his school exams without ever impressing any of his teachers as being a good or even a second-rate brain. Doggedness was everything: doggy perseverance in search of affection, and wild dog snarling when things went wrong. Collis could brashly give offence and expect it to be taken as a joke; but offend Collis, and you found yourself backing away from something crouching and baring its teeth, ready for trouble and sure in advance that it has been deliberately directed at him and nobody else. Wonderful if he was on your side, but frightening if you were on the receiving end of one of his attacks. Collis used his capabilities unrestrainedly, intuitively, at full stretch; and could take virtually any punishment he got in return without wincing. But not mental punishment: not what he was suffering from the thought of that black lad lying in hospital right at this minute.

So Miller had had to endure an Irish joke. What about hammering Collis with a joke about blacks . . .?

It was beneath consideration.

They made quite a team. Detective Inspector Mackie had spotted the potential only a few days after two of his best operators had been killed in a high-speed chase. Neither Miller nor Collis admitted to any instinctive respect for each other, let alone a mutual liking. But Mackie had sensed what counted, and they knew Mackie was a good judge, and it was never mentioned. Mutually taking the mickey was better than agreeing with Mackie's judgment.

Miller shifted in his seat and yawned.

The door they had been watching opened, and a man came out. Two more emerged from the shadows and scurried into the house.

Collis began a tuneless whistling.

After another five minutes Miller could stand no more. 'Let's visit.'

'Everybody else is doing just that,' Collis agreed.

They got out of the car and headed across the street to the door of the house. The glow of a red light bulb warmed the grotty wallpaper immediately inside, concealing the stains and rents in the stair carpet.

They plodded upstairs. It was all routine; all dull and depressing; nothing to do with visions of our heroic boys in blue (or, in Collis's case, in a black leather jacket and in Miller's a sports jacket which had seen better days); nothing, really, to do with anybody except a handful of dismal little people who wanted only to be left alone to their grubby little devices.

There was an outburst of giggling from a door along the first landing. Collis marched up to it, knocked loudly, and led the way in.

The bedroom was suffused with what might have been planned as intimate lighting: that is to say, there were two bedside lamps with nauseating purple shades. As the two sergeants barged in, a middle-aged woman sat up in anger, and in nothing else. Two men, similarly naked, bobbed up on either side like a brace of jacks-in-the-box. The tableau could have made an excellent subject for a jolly seaside postcard. But none of the three looked jolly. A few minutes ago maybe they had been laughing their heads off, but not right now.

'And what do you two want?' demanded the woman, cold and deadly.

'Mrs Henderson?' Collis was equally cold but more polite. 'Just wondered if you could oblige with a few words.'

'You'll get a few bloody words all right if you don't –'

'I'm afraid I'll have to take up a little bit of your time.'

'You can just turn yourselves around, both of you,' said Mrs Henderson, 'and bugger off out.'

'Mrs Henderson.' Miller took his turn. 'You're going to have to accompany us to the local police station.'

His voice was immediately more impressive than Collis's had been. She glared at him, but for the first time plucked the edge of the sheet over her breasts. 'For what reason? Why?'

'If you're demanding reasons,' said Collis snappishly, 'we might also do you for wasting police time.'

She clambered over one of the men, thumped off the edge of the bed, and closed the door with a resounding slam as she went into the bathroom.

Miller nodded at Collis. 'I'll spin the drum.'

As he headed out to search the place, Collis propped himself against the wall and surveyed the two men sitting sheepishly upright in bed. Pretty fat sheep they were: so flabby that Collis could almost persuade himself that his own diet had been a miracle cure and he really had nothing to worry about after all.

'Quite chilly for the time of year,' he said affably.

The man on the right scratched his hip. 'I wouldn't say that.'

'What would you say?'

'I'd say sod off out of here. It isn't illegal in this country to seek the comfort of a woman.'

'That's a new one. I haven't heard that. What's that supposed to mean – "the comfort of a woman"?'

Neither of them replied. Collis could hear the creak of the stairs as Miller went up, thumping about overhead; and then he was on his way down again.

Mrs Henderson erupted from the bathroom in a garish floral housecoat. 'All right, where's the other one? Search warrant – let's see it, if he's on the premises snooping around.'

She reached for her handbag. Miller, coming in, spotted the plastic envelope of white powder that had been hidden beneath it. Before Mrs Henderson could realize her mistake he had snatched it up and sniffed the contents.

'Heroin.' He and Collis exchanged glances. In their time both of them had picked up dying teenage junkies, driven them to hospital, and felt sick for a long time afterwards. Miller dropped all pretence at politeness. 'We heard you'd become a fence in a big way,' he said icily to the woman. 'Didn't realize it included this filth. You're nicked.'

'I never seen that plastic bag till you got at it. I don't know what's in it.'

Collis dragged the blanket and sheet off the two men and waved at their pin-striped business suits draped neatly over the backs of the bedside chairs. 'Get dressed.'

'You've no right to talk to us like that. I warn you, there are some people –'

'That wasn't on the table before them two came in,' said Mrs Henderson wildly. 'So you direct your bastard questions where they belong.'

'Do yourself a favour,' said Collis. 'Stop shouting.'

The men struggled, mumbling and cursing, into their clothes, while Collis watched contemptuously. Miller did not for a second stop watching Mrs Henderson. Mounting hatred twisted his lower lip.

'Right. Downstairs, the lot of you.'

'I never saw that stuff, you can't prove –'

'Stop shouting,' said Collis again, opening the bedroom door and gesturing towards the stairs. 'Start thinking about what you're going to say in your statement.' They jostled each other all the way down. 'In the car, darling.'

'Don't call me darling.'

As they slid into the police car, the R/T on the fascia sprang into life.

'MP, MP to central four-four. Central four-four.'

Squashed against the offside rear door, one of the two businessmen whined: 'My lawyer's partner is a Knight of the Realm. You get that? A Knight of the Realm. He'll sort you out.'

'Yeah, yeah,' said Collis indifferently.

'Central four-four. Report my signal.'

Miller took up the handset. 'Central four-four receiving.
'Chief Inspector Haldane message – return urgently.'

'Received. We're on our way. Ten minutes. Central four-four out.'

Collis started the car. A summons to Detective Chief Inspector Haldane's office always meant business – and not the kind of business these two slobs with Mrs Henderson practised. What was it going to be this time?

There were a dozen senior officers in the C11 projector room when the Deputy Assistant Commissioner Crime joined them and signalled the go-ahead. Superintendent Costigan of C11, Criminal Intelligence Branch, stood and addressed the group.

'We're looking to try and identify a face. The face is moving in some celebrated company. We have some photographs by one of our detective sergeants, Jock Willis. He's one of a team on Target Person Surveillance. Subject is a Harold Aitken who does not feature in this opera. But out of the Aitken TPS we get a face with no name. And we'd like to know a bit more. Lights, somebody.'

As the lights went off, Costigan began inserting slides into the projector. On the far wall there swam into view a bald city type in his way from a bank towards a Rolls at the kerb.

'Harold Aitken. Initial surveillance subject. He's currently *the* porn video baron. There are some people being killed in that business. Thus our recently renewed interest.'

He offered a couple more views of Aitken, including one of him falling down the steps of the Athenæum. Presumably it followed a liquid lunch within those august portals. Then came quite a few angles of no apparent significance, including one showing the back of two men's heads.

'Wait for the reverse,' said Jock Willis from the back of the room.

There was a faint whistle. Two or three officers present

recognized the face with Aitken. David Monroe had passed across their field of view a number of times, always involved with the wrong sort of people but somehow never getting his hands too obviously dirty. There was always somebody like that on the fringe – and you could never be sure just how much further in he might be involved.

A chartered accountant with a public school background, Monroe was undeniably bright. He had made a lot of money in his time. It was on the record that he had also lost a lot of it in the mid-seventies property crash. But somehow he was soon looking prosperous again. The only time the Yard had ever had a collar on him was when he was blundering about a bit on his own: twenty-two months for minor fraud, out of an active life of thirty years. Since then he had climbed back – on whose shoulders? The word was that he liked to be around violence and violent men: that was how he got his kicks. But there was never anything you could pin on him. By now he must be a millionaire. A career villain, all right: the wealth was obvious, the career a success story ... but how could you establish the villainy?

'The reason for our get-together,' Costigan was saying, 'is this next gent coming up. I'd like you to take a good long look. Let's say Aitken is X, Monroe is Y. Then who's this – who's Z?'

A series of slides showed Monroe with a well-dressed man in his fifties, looking powerful and at home in a number of London locations. He rarely smiled. Something about him said that he didn't need to. In one sequence, Monroe was getting out of the front of a chauffeur-driven Daimler to open the rear door while the man got out.

'Note that,' said Costigan. 'Our wealthy friend Monroe gets out and opens the car door for this gent. Implicitly Mr Z is more important than Monroe. So does anyone have the faintest idea who he is?'

'A foreigner?'

'Does he look foreign?'

'I got near enough,' Jock Willis volunteered, 'to hear Mr Z speak. London accent.'

'Back from abroad?' suggested the man beside him. 'A Spanish refugee?'

'Lights, please.' As they blinked in the brightness, Costigan looked around. 'Anybody, any ideas?'

'A yachtsman?'

'Costa Brava . . .?'

'Could be.'

'What do you mean, a yachtsman?' asked the DACC.

'Costa Brava villains, like Ronnie Knight, bought huge villas, lived high profile. That's your second division thug. The first division, the masterminds, have ocean-going yachts. Moor them in little bays. Move along when the mood takes them. Cops come to look them over, they put to sea, move to another bay. Always mobile.'

'The Spanish coast –'

'Portugal's posher,' commented DI Mackie, sitting at Haldane's left.

'All right, Portugal, maybe. Spain or Portugal, it's a possibility.'

'Would the Spanish police be able to check this face?' asked the DACC. 'Or the Portuguese?'

Costigan pursed his lips. 'I think that's the point, sir. That's really what we're up against: no one knows who these yachtsmen are. And none of us has a glimmering about *this* one, or even if he's in that category anyway.'

Mutual co-operation was promised. Inter-departmental liaison was confirmed. But when Haldane and Mackie left the C11 offices they were not much the wiser. And right now the DCI had other things on his mind.

'Are Miller and Collis back yet?'

'I'll check, guv.'

The detective inspector was on his way past the lift as the doors opened and the two sergeants came out. He nodded them threateningly along the corridor towards Haldane's office. Mackie always looked threatening: not aggressively but dourly so, as if the best of tidings could somehow get poisoned and transformed into bad news within his head. He showed at all times a sort of mocking world-weariness, expressed in odd vocal inflections and the pessimism of his saturnine features. The streaks of grey in his hair were of the same hard tone as a battleship.

'What's it all about, guv?'

'You'll find out.' The menace was implicit. Then Mackie relented slightly. 'What were you at when you were called back?'

'Mrs Henderson,' said Collis. 'Spun the drum. No gear, but looks like a quarter pound of heroin.'

'*Is*,' said Miller flatly, 'not looks like.'

'Full-time business,' Mackie queried, 'or pleasure?'

'Don't know. Slung the bodies to the Drug Squad. They seemed keen to have her.'

'Not for sex, I trust?'

'They're funny people,' said Collis chirpily.

'So no evidence she's a big fence?'

'No evidence,' said Miller.

DCI Haldane was on the phone as they went in. He finished his call abruptly and looked up at them across his desk.

'Heard you were assigned to a whore. How was she?'

'Surprise package. Quarter pound of heroin. Nothing else.'

'Is she an addict?'

'No form that we heard of. Maybe something'll be turned up.'

'Sit down.' Haldane waved towards two hardbacked chairs. 'I've got another heroin story for you.'

Miller and Collis sat down. Mackie edged towards a more comfortable chair beside the desk.

Haldane went on: 'Someone's been phoning me up. Direct dial car phone. And before you ask, no, we haven't. There are more than twelve thousand licensed direct dial car phones in the UK. This informer's given us seven names. Drug couriers. Each of them has been arrested at Heathrow carrying substantial quantities of drugs. To date, street value in the region of nineteen million. The first name was eight days ago – a Beiruti in from Amsterdam. Second name twenty-four hours later, a bloke from the Seychelles in from Switzerland.'

'This wasn't in the *Sun*, guv,' observed Collis.

'We've kept it out of Fleet Street.'

'Why,' asked Miller thoughtfully, 'phone the fourth floor?'

Haldane nodded appreciation of the point. 'I get the sense that the caller knows the Squad Office. Maybe past dealings with the Sweeney.'

'All lifted, the seven?'

'Drug Squad get the bodies, although they'll allow us interrogation. So you two, off to Heathrow. Your contact' – he consulted a note on the desk before him – 'is a Brian Salter, HM Customs. All these guys are non-UK residents. Some of them have never set foot in England before. Yet as each was arrested, each produced the name of a top London lawyer. Why? Where do they get it from? The latest guy has asked for Coren and Lehmann, solicitors. Make sense of it.'

As the three men got up and headed out, Haldane called Miller back.

'Yes, guv?'

'Close the door a minute.' When Miller had done so, Haldane went on brusquely: 'Nineteen million from seven into Heathrow. No indication that's the last phone call we'll be getting. So let's see a bit of intelligence. One cock-up, and we could scare them all off. Use your mind.'

'Right, guv.'

'And see your oppo behaves himself.' Haldane flicked his tongue against his teeth. 'Come to think of it, you'd better go out in two cars. If you have to split up to follow any interesting leads, okay. But if it's a one-man job, you be that one man. Send Collis back here.'

'Right, guv.'

'Names and flight numbers,' Haldane mused. 'And every one a multi-million-pound collar. It sounds mad. Damn it, it *is* mad. And yet somewhere there's got to be a bloody good reason for it.'

He waved a dismissive hand.

It was difficult to disagree with the DCI. The bits and pieces so far added up to nothing but madness; or, at the very least, some way-out weirdness.

Salter of the Drug Squad was waiting for the two of them to roll up at the Customs and Excise building. His handshake was brief and not exactly welcoming. 'I don't know what you lot are doing on this.'

'Don't ask me, brother,' said Collis airily.

'I am asking you, brother.'

'Ask our guv'nor.'

Salter grimaced, and without another word led them along a deserted corridor to a large, bleak room with a scattering of chairs and trestle tables. There were only two occupants: a dejected-looking man with a complexion which could have come from any one of several countries in the Middle East, and a head which dipped lower as they approached; and a watchful security man with his back braced against one wall as if on the alert, waiting for an excuse to fling himself forward.

'He's not been charged?' Miller asked Salter.

'He's got a brief he wants to call. Just like the rest of 'em. Doing the ignorant "no understandee" act. Six in hand, one the last week, all the same.' As they stopped a few feet from the man squatting on the chair, Salter said in an undertone: 'I'm told you're to have five minutes.'

Miller looked down at the bowed head. 'Mr Khalid Khan?'

The man nodded.

'You speak English?' When Khan nodded again, Miller said: 'Cup of tea?'

'Yes, sir.' It was little more than a whisper. 'Coffee?'

'Milk and sugar?'

'No, sir.'

Miller glanced at Salter. 'Can we get him some coffee?'

'Machine's broke.' Salter turned away and walked off.

'There's no coffee,' said Miller. He held his fire for long enough to start the man's knuckles tightening and whitening. Then he said levelly: 'You were informed on. You know what "informed" means?'

'Yes, sir.'

'You're going to go down for a minimum ten years. It's computable. Know what that means? It means sentence relates to the quantity you brought in.' Miller leaned over Khalid Khan and dropped his voice soothingly, coaxingly. 'Now, somebody talked about you. We want you to do yourself a good turn. We want you to think who that somebody might be – and talk about him.'

'You must allow me to talk to lawyer.'

'Have you been in this country before, Mr Khan?'

'No, sir.'

'You seem to know our laws.'

'Sir?'

Collis edged in beside Miller, less restrained, biting his words out. 'Who provided you with the name of a leading lawyer? Where did you get the name from? Did they brief you because they knew all along that you'd be arrested?'

There was silence.

'Listen,' said Miller. 'We don't have to tell you this, but we will. Six other people who've arrived in this airport carrying heroin in the last seven days – information about them has been given to us just as their planes touched down. Right on the dot, every time. We're asking you for any ideas you might have. Our guess is that the man who sent you into this country with heroin is the man who – for God knows what bizarre reason – shopped you. And six others like you.'

'Look at us when we're talking to you,' raged Collis.

Khalid Khan raised his head. Whatever emotions his

tightly interlaced hands were betraying, his face expressed nothing at all.

They turned away, seeing Salter waiting for them at the end of the room.

Collis said wonderingly: 'What sort of wheeler-dealer would think up anything as perverse as that?'

4 Being back in town was a good feeling, a great feeling for George Payne if not for everyone else. Planning the return had been like planning a holiday, making cosy arrangements well ahead and sorting out a few entertaining itineraries. Payne was not the kind of man to relax on holidays: there had been enough of that sunny indolence these last six years. This was what they called a working holiday. There were two or three people to drop in on, or to drop into something; a few items to be tidied up or settled up. Payne visited a few old haunts and steered prudently clear of others. So far there was little chance of anyone fitting his name and his face together. That was how he intended to keep it until, later, flattering rumours might link the two of them.

Neither the police nor the gossip columnists had any reason to know anything about the Mr George Hanrahan who had booked into a suite at the London Embassy Hotel. It was a plush environment, such as he had grown accustomed to; yet there was another venue to visit which would give him much greater satisfaction, offer more enjoyment than most of his other accomplishments laid end to end. Opening *The Times* under the dim, dusty light of the few bulbs still functioning in the wall brackets, he sprawled back and savoured the dusty air, the taste of powdered cinema seat coverings and plaster.

Years back, when little Georgie Payne had been only a nipper, he had lived for those twice-weekly visits to the Odeon, Dalston. He had sworn that one fine day he would have one just like it for his very own. And here he was, settled in the stalls of his own cinema as if waiting for the big feature. Not that he would have been reading *The Times* business pages in those days. And not that there was going to be a big feature here today. Not on the screen,

46

anyway. He had acquired the place only because lack of business had forced it to close down; and before long he would be finding ways of having it demolished and replaced by some more profitable property. All the same, of all the places he owned, this was the most heart-warming.

A swing door at the back of the stalls flapped to and fro. Footsteps came down the slope of the aisle to the end of his row. It wasn't the ice-cream girl. In a way he would have preferred that. Still, he could work up an appetite for what was about to be presented to him.

'Here we are, Mr Payne,' said Hanley.

Colin Ettrick had brought three of his heftiest minders with him. They were sitting hunched in a menacing group one row back. Payne folded his newspaper and with a leisurely movement put it on the seat beside him. He had no need to display his own muscle too openly. They were there in the shadows if he had to call on them in a hurry; but he thought it unlikely that he would even have to raise his voice.

'All right, George.' Colin Ettrick's arms dangled by his sides, but no one would have mistaken that for a state of relaxation. 'What d'you want to talk about?'

Hanley cleared his throat. It was no more a hospitable sound than Ettrick's greeting had been. 'Six years away in the sunshine,' he growled, 'and that's all you've got to say when Mr Payne gets back? Aren't you going to say how much we've all missed him?'

Ettrick ignored him and stared questioningly at Payne. His eyes were pale and his lips even paler, apparently bloodless. He could have been a very sick young man in need of a transfusion and a course in body-building; but if he was sick it was only in what passed for his mind, and he was not that much younger than George Payne. He said: 'How long you been back?'

'Two months.'

'I didn't know.' Ettrick's lips writhed a slow dance, one

over the other. He was plainly assessing the time and the possibilities, adding up just how much Payne might have accomplished within two surreptitious months. 'That long. . . .'

'I've been occupied.'

'I'm also busy, George.'

They eyed each other. Ettrick clearly thought he was a dab hand at sizing things up, clever at sparring. Payne let him bathe in his own self-satisfaction for a long, long twenty seconds, then said: 'Yes, a bit busy, Colin. We have to talk about that.'

'Yeah, that was always your thing, George – lots of chat.'

Ettrick lowered himself condescendingly into the next seat. One of the other seats at the back of the stalls creaked ominously as a dark, broad shadow got up.

'Was it?' Payne kept the mood quiet, throttled down. 'My associates are saying that you've been taking up with some wrong faces. All right, London's a big manor. Biggest in the world. Plenty of room for every race, colour and creed. But' – he leaned suddenly towards Ettrick, his chin thrusting and his voice thrusting with it – 'not Sicilians. Not the sodding mob, Colin.' He waited. When Ettrick made no response he said: 'Why are you talking to them?'

'You were a long time on your boat. It's all different nowadays. A geezer knocks off a building society in the Finchley Road for a couple of grand, he takes the money and buys heroin. And he deals. Heroin, cocaine – they're the new currency. Worldwide. But the notes are still printed in Palermo, if you get my meaning.'

'I get your meaning. And I can supply anything you want.' Payne was mild and low-key again. 'You want a ton of grade one Pakistani heroin? I'll get it for you faster, cheaper than those Sicilian wankers.'

'Oh, yes?'

'I don't want them, or their money, or their nasty habits, in London. If I get any more reports of you consorting with them, I'll have to do something about it.'

Colin Ettrick leaned back as if giving this some earnest thought. Then he got up and slowly headed back along the row towards the aisle. His hoods closed in around him as he strolled to the exit, looking back just once.

'And that's all you've got to say? You must have been a big fish in a little pool on your Costa-whatever-it-was. It isn't that you got too big, George. You've got too fat. It had to be a prospect that sooner or later someone would cut you down to size.'

The swing door flapped again once, twice, three times.

Monroe half rose from his unobtrusive place on the far side of the stalls and looked back towards Payne, waiting for instructions, or a reaction.

Payne said: 'We'll have to roll up one of his Italian friends. As an example. Just for starters.'

'That Dacre bloke. He's always neat.' Monroe's close-set eyes gleamed in the twilight of the cinema. He could never have summoned up the guts to be violent himself, but he loved to be around violence and to set it in motion.

Payne nodded approval.

Monroe was on his feet. There was a slight, shrill tremor in his tone. 'If we take out one of Ettrick's raviolis, it's going to be like *High Noon*.'

It was high time, thought Payne, to give Monroe some sobering routine work to do before he got too excited. There were plenty of routine details to be attended to. Keep the man occupied, thought Payne warily, and make it clear who's giving the orders.

'All right, Dacre it is. But before that, I want you to check on the van. Height, weight, every last little thing.'

'It's in good hands. You can trust –'

'I trust you,' said Payne blandly, 'to be down there every day until *the* day. Checking it until you're sure it's going to work. If it falls apart when it hits, everything else falls apart.'

For a moment it looked as if Monroe were about to

assert himself and start arguing. Then he thought better of it, and left.

It was no good saying that everything had been checked and rechecked. There might still be one last hitch, one unforeseen weakness. Nobody in George Payne's little empire was going to relax until it was all over.

Denton had measured the height of the giant DAF turbo-charged diesel at least a dozen times, and compared it with a polaroid of a mini-van up against the very wall they had set their sights. Measuring the height of the mini-van and wall as a percentage, he had got the assessment out at three feet nine to three feet ten. The hard linings and the shocks had been organised. The windscreen had been replaced with perspex, and then a couple of bars added to protect the driver. The way the thing was built, the velocity and weight . . . it was going to be one hell of an impact. But Denton was confident. Denton was so confident of his own know-how that he turned pretty nasty when Ennis raised a doubt.

'I'd like to add a little health hazard warning. I was once in a heavy vehicle doing a runner, we hit a hump-backed bridge – a bit like the ramp we're talking about right now. We went up . . . and when we came down we lost all our tyres.'

'The tyres will hold,' Denton growled.

'You think so?'

'I know so.'

'Just offering. In case they weren't in your calculations.'

Denton waved his oxy-acetylene torch to and fro. Any minute now it threatened to become a flame-thrower. 'There's nothing we haven't bloody well calculated.'

All the same, Payne wanted Monroe down there every day at regular intervals, keeping an eye on progress and making it clear that at the same time he was keeping an eye on each and every man in the team. From now on it might be sound policy, thought Payne, to have them all put up in one of his lesser hotels, with orders not to leave it. Keep them together and minimize the risk of any free-lance escapades: no falling into petty temptation just before the off. It was not unreasonable to ask the lot of them to put up with a few minor inconveniences for a very brief period. After all, what was going to follow would be quite an historic occasion: bags of profit and a great swell of subterranean prestige through the whole manor.

Payne sensed it was time to turn his attention to a deal with Anthony Webb, MP. While he was back in town he might as well use his leisure moments to put the seal on some of his other ventures, rather than leave it to middlemen without quite his personal clout.

Tony Webb was none too pleased to learn that George Payne was back on the scene. After his first hesitation on the phone he began to gush, but the hesitation had been enough: Payne could visualize the expression on the man's face and heard the momentary, protesting intake of breath. But there was to be no protest, no argument: Payne wanted them to meet, so meet they would.

'Five years, George.' Webb might have added that it didn't seem a day too much. He added no such thing, but George Payne got the echo of it and allowed himself a rare, complacent smile. They all thought that once they had got away with something, paying a small price for a big favour, there would never be a further reckoning. Even the most cunning wheeler-dealers and politicians rarely foresaw the extra tax they might sooner or later have to fork out on the dividends they had received.

'I could come and have lunch with you at the House, maybe,' said Payne.

The resonance of fear grew stronger. 'It's not an easy place to talk, George. You know what they're like – everybody staring over everybody's shoulder to see what's happening and who to suck up to.'

'Your club, then? I hear you've moved up a grade in the

ratings. On the committee of the Carlton now – isn't that so?'

'I –'

'All right, Tony.' Payne let him off the hook. In his own interests he was in fact happy to keep a low profile. 'What's the best place in Chelsea since some wayward character shot up our old rendezvous?'

The wayward character, as it happened, had been Hanley's predecessor, who had himself subsequently been obliterated by a vengeful family who objected to the protection set-up and to the summary demolition of a relative's premises; but Webb did not know that, and it would serve little purpose to let him know.

'There's a quiet little place down Wilton Street. Only been there a few months – not too many people have got on to it yet.'

'Called?'

'La Cabriole.'

'Noon?'

'I'm not sure I can make it that early.'

'Quarter past, then,' said Payne amenably. 'Give you time to digest everything before you show up at the House.'

It was all so easy. It had been smooth and easy before he left for Spain and Portugal, and it was going to be just as simple again. As a taxpayer Payne might have felt righteously indignant at the way in which Parliament allowed its members to get away with undeclared earnings from pressure groups of every hue instead of concentrating on the true needs of the communities they claimed to represent. But in the first place George Payne took care to pay no UK tax whatsoever; and in the second place he greatly appreciated the facilities which were made so readily available to him. He did not bother with the everyday retainers paid to 'consultants' who listed their status in the Register of Interests. Payne went in for 'sweeteners', which cost a lot more but were not registered.

And along with the sweeteners there often went something less sweet – something which could leave a nasty aftertaste, a dryness in the mouth, the belated knowledge that something had gone too far . . . and was likely to go a whole lot further.

Tony Webb had blissfully believed for these last five years that he had gone to the limit without being caught and was free of any more commitments.

Tony Webb had another think coming.

'Who was that, darling?'

Stella had come into the room with a large vase of flowers newly culled from the garden, set it down next to the photograph of Simon and Jessica, and tweaked four of the stems back into the right conformation.

'Damned nuisance,' said Webb. 'Some awkward cuss from Land Registry who's raising questions with the Department. The minister wants me to calm him down – over lunch, would you believe?'

'But I thought you were coming to Harrods with me to sort out that mix-up over Jessica's riding tackle. *And* you promised *me* lunch.'

'It's a bind, but you know how these things are.'

'Oh, do I not!'

But her smile was amiable enough. Brought up in a household where it was taken for granted that commercial and political manipulation of the country in its own best interests took precedence over any personal considerations, Stella had found no difficulty in adjusting to the lifestyle of an ambitious MP. Indeed, if his ambitions ever showed any sign of flagging she would be the first to urge him on. Like other political wives and hostesses she had produced a representative sample of the right breed of children, who went to the right sort of school; and with help from her father a suitable family home had been established in a listed mansion in the south-west corner of Anthony Webb's Surrey constituency. It was a safe buy. The likelihood of their having to move was remote: few safer Tory seats existed.

She had never suspected how close he had come to leaving the House, the London flat and the Surrey mansion – leaving her and the children. . . .

Absences because of his career she understood and forgave. Permanent, irrevocable absence with Beth she would neither have understood nor forgiven. Neither would her father. Which meant that also the Party would not forgive him. When Sir Edmund Eames disapproved of something, even the Cabinet felt the repercussions.

At the brink, Webb had looked back and seen what he was about to lose. It was too late to turn back, yet too awful to have to live up to his word and go on. There was no help anywhere. Until George Payne intervened. If he *did* intervene.

It had never been openly avowed. Webb had carefully not thought about it during that subsequent six months, and as time went by found it easier to wipe the whole question from his mind. There were so many other, more immediate concerns. That old one was forgotten. Self-reproach would not help him to face the future. He really learned to keep Beth out of his mind altogether until the sound of Payne's voice on the phone stirred up old echoes.

It had all begun in the days when he was a parliamentary private secretary to the Ministry of Transport, concerned primarily with overseeing of local authority transport planning. Already he had been earmarked – and knew it – as a promising young man. His marriage to Stella and the backing of her father, Sir Edmund, chairman of the local Conservative Party and managing director of a large technical publishing group, had certainly done nothing to diminish his chances.

Doubts took a few years to insinuate themselves into his mind: doubts about a career which owed so much to his wife's background and her father's influence, awareness that so many people knew about it, and doubts about his ability to go on for all his working life living up to her expectations. It would all take unfailing, exhausting concentration. All work and no play. . . .

Relaxation and laughter came not with Stella but with Beth. It began with admiration and unpremeditatedly changed to something deeper. She was the brightest and most efficient of the girls in the Statistics department. Sound, sensible and reliable, she saved him a lot of administrative headaches; and continued to be undemanding when at last he took her into bed and, on one occasion after another, took her away on trips that had nothing to do with transports other than their own. Her only demands were physical: sobbing, thrashing in his arms like a wild thing, as if to make up for all the hours and days of impersonal memoranda and files and statistics.

She never went so far as to ask him to marry her. But the two of them were inexorably being drawn towards that whirlpool.

It wouldn't work.

It would not work without enough money to make the break. There would be no Parliamentary future for him if he went off with Beth. So he must find a way of stacking something up to guarantee independence – and comfort.

George Payne came on the scene.

How had Payne come to pick on him, just at this time? It took Webb many sleepless hours to realize the magnitude of Payne's resources, the information service that fed him with details of a weakness here, a vulnerable spot there, so that he could select the right man for any of his purposes at exactly the right time.

From preliminary talks there surfaced a proposition, not too bluntly revealed at first, concerning some building developments between the South Bank and the South Circular Road. The GLC had approved a plan to reorientate the road patterns around two roundabouts to relieve traffic congestion and allow for a swathe of dual carriageway through a cluster of festering old terraces of substandard housing and shops. Payne's sniffer dogs had got wind of the proposals and, through a network of theoretically unconnected associates, bought up some of the key properties. By the time the local authority came to discuss purchase prices under 'land for planning permission' formulae, costs were deliciously muddled. Rather than flounder through squabbles over notices to treat and compulsory purchase orders, with all the attendant bad publicity and the expensive delays caused by a protracted public enquiry, it would surely make sense to reach an agreement with the major owner – namely, George Payne.

Not that Payne wanted his name bandied around. What he did want was Anthony Webb's influence within his Department to nudge forward a compromise. Rationalization of the road configurations could go ahead after the purchase of Payne's properties at a nominal figure – provided Payne was granted permission to demolish the remainder and rebuild on a denser plot ratio than was normally permissible. It was a deal that needed wrapping up in impenetrable governmental terminology, and publicity had to be avoided until it was too late for groups such as the Fine Art Commission to register formal objections.

In consideration of Tony Webb's help in ironing out the problems there would be a gift of shares in a design group whose holding company also controlled the property development company through two removes. A little portion of the equity in return for favours received: what could be fairer, in this competitive world?

The income would be sufficient to keep Tony Webb and his Beth, if not in the style to which he had become accustomed, at any rate in greater comfort than many an impetuous eloping couple.

As plans for the deal and plans for going off with Beth were being finalized, two things happened. One was that Beth grew more and more tearful and lost her usual self-possession. She felt sick inside about the whole thing. She wanted to rush their departure, be done with it, make a clean break and fight out the petty conflicts later. Twice she phoned him at the flat when Stella was there, and once in the country. He had to make up stories on the spur of the moment, and rage at Beth later. The hours he spent with her were increasingly devoted to recriminations and confused promises and appeals. The final crunch came when she told him she was pregnant.

The second thing to upset the precarious balance was the intimation, brought into conversation as subtly and deviously as all such things were, that he was in line for an important transfer to the Department of the Environment.

All this was, of course, now only a dream of what might have been. He had made his decision. Or Beth had made it imperative that a decision should be made.

At one of their meetings George Payne said: 'For a man who's getting everything the way he wanted it, you're looking pretty bloody miserable.'

'Everything?'

'What else did you have in mind?'

Escape: that was all he had in mind. Escape from an impossible situation, with unbearable consequences which-ever way he jumped. It came out in a rush, snarling and angry, blaming Payne as much as anyone for the mess he was in, while Payne's face went dark with one of his slow, implacable rages, and then cleared miraculously. What triggered Payne's sudden benevolence was a line or two about Tony Webb's lost prospects, of the promotion he would now never have.

'How interesting! Such possibilities opening up, just when we might need them.'

Planning permission was rushed through in the form Payne had dictated. It made such good sense. The Select Committee issued their ruling, and it was only after acceptance had been hastily confirmed that two Opposition members and one national newspaper with a blazoned 'Exclusive' header proclaimed that two essential documents had gone astray and never been presented. These dissenting views had totally contradicted the supposition on which permission had been granted, and had presented evidence to refute those suppositions. What had happened to them?

It was a tidy get-out, fitting neatly into the pattern of Webb's fatalistic progress. Unable to explain how such documents could have been mislaid within his Department, he gallantly offered his resignation and took full blame for whatever silly errors some nameless subordinate might have made.

Webb's minister said that he was unwilling to accept the resignation. The Prime Minister expressed dismay. Somewhere behind the Prime Minister and other stalwarts, behind all the shadowy doubts about inconsistencies in the official story, stood Sir Edmund Eames and his staunch team. To Webb's mingled delight and discomfiture, a backlash of civil service admiration for his integrity in shouldering the blame for what everyone in the Department felt must be the blunder of one of their own colleagues reinforced his public image. The resignation fluttered in the air like a proud, defiant banner. Party and public demanded that it should be hauled down.

On the night of the greatest turmoil, with an entire television programme devoted to the question of departmental and ministerial responsibility, Stella Webb came to her husband in a naked adoration more lustful than she had ever shown him before. Hot and moist and possessive, she locked him between her legs in what might have been an unspoken threat to crush him rather than let him go. Yet there was no way she could have guessed how close he was to escaping.

The next day he did not go to Beth to sort out the last details of their flight – timing, the hotel where they would stay for a few days, how they would dodge the press and TV cameras, and then what they would say when the media caught up with them. Instead he added up credits and debits; and knew he was about to make a fool of himself.

Too late. There was neither reason nor dignity in squatting here in a maudlin mire of regrets. He had to summon up the courage to tell Stella and be on his way.

Tomorrow he would tell her.

That following morning he heard the news: first vaguely on the Radio 4 *Today* programme as an inexplicable accident on the M3, and then as a side issue in a telephone call from the Department. Beth had been driving out of London that previous evening, heading south-west. 'Not on her way to you with any papers or anything you'd asked for, Tony?' No, most decidedly not. Well, it had only been in his general direction: just a possible lead they'd had.

One witness travelling in the opposite direction said that a car driving only on sidelights had clipped Beth's MG at an angle and somehow seemed locked with it, unable to free itself, until she was driven off the road. There was a police search, an appeal for information. The search went nowhere; the appeal produced, as usual, half a dozen false trails and no more.

Beth was dead. No driver ever came forward to admit liability or give evidence of someone who might have been implicated.

For some reason, which he did not dare confess even to himself, Tony Webb put off contacting George Payne. If there was anything to know, he refused to know it. The accusation that made him sweat in the middle of the night was one he had to reject, smother, deny and deny. Nothing so monstrous could conceivably have happened.

Payne summoned him.

Webb refused to ask outright. He listened to Payne's glib, concise summing-up of the current state of play, and put a brave face on his protest: 'Out of the question. I couldn't go into this new job with any risk of being linked with dividends rolling in from –'

'Already fixed. On top of all the other safeguards, it all goes through a bank in Jersey.'

'One whisper of an undeclared interest, and –'

'If you think the Swiss are good at stifling financial whispers,' said Payne comfortingly, 'you don't know what clever little clams they've got in Jersey.'

'I'm not sure I'm prepared to go on. After all that's happened. . . .' He realized that over the last few minutes he had revealingly been putting things in the wrong order. He had virtually admitted that he proposed to go on – and up. 'Look,' he flagellated himself, 'you know about Beth.'

'I did hear. I'm sorry about that, for your sake. Or maybe for your sake I shouldn't be too sorry.'

'What do you mean? You know damn well we meant to –'

'I know you didn't look too happy about it. About any of it.'

'What was between Beth and me, that was nothing do to with you.'

'Never suggested it was. But face up to it, Tony – you were really going off the boil so far as she was concerned. In the end you might say fate turned up trumps. Without you having to do a single damn thing about it.' Payne wrinkled his nose in a benevolent grimace. 'I guess she was on her way to see you that night. And that wouldn't have been a whole heap of fun, would it? Fate stepped in –'

'Who did you say stepped in?'

'It's a useful get-out,' said Payne. 'Keep telling it to yourself that way: fate.'

'I wasn't asking for a get-out.'

'Weren't you?'

Webb waited a shuddering eternity and then said: 'I can't think straight. I just want to get out of all this. Out of everything.'

'No, you don't. You go straight to your new job. And collect a few thousand as you pass "Go".'

'I've tendered my resignation.'

'Which they won't accept.'

Payne was proved right. Mr Anthony Webb's integrity in tendering his resignation seemed to fit him even more worthily for his new post in the Department of the Environment. After withdrawing his resignation gracefully, under pressure, he carved out for himself an illustrious niche as Under-Secretary of State with expert knowledge of planning land use policy. His wife was, as ever, a pillar of strength in London and in the constituency. His father-in-law did not so much murmur into influential ears as bark orders into them. Tony and Stella dined at Number 10 three times in two months.

And there was that three weeks' holiday in Portugal, discreetly arranged by a grateful Mr George Payne, though yet again the name was never mentioned. A second honeymoon, you might have called it: a chance to slough off memories of that silly woman who might have ruined his life and thereby damaged the country for which he so assiduously worked. Stella was once more startlingly, shamelessly ardent – for a few nights, anyway. After that she went back, without his being too disconcerted, to the role of helpmeet and political hostess.

And now, across the table, Payne was saying: 'My Mr Monroe tells me there has been some hold-up with our new hotel.'

'I don't think I know about that. Not my pigeon. I don't handle every building in the country, old chap.'

'Didn't suppose you would. But I'm sure you know who does. This particular erection is my little venture down river from Tower Bridge.'

'Oh, that one. I think I did hear something.'

'I thought you might have.'

'But George, honestly, I don't have much of an idea what's going on in that sector. Can't say much off the cuff, anyway.'

'Perhaps you're in a position to *get* an idea?' Payne watched the wine waiter pour Pichon-Longueville into his glass, sniffed appreciatively, thought of the local Portuguese wines and knew how glad he was to be back in London.

When the waiter had backed away, he went on: 'Plans inspectorate – is that the right little box? Some riverside conservationist crackpots muddying up the waters?'

'Things aren't as easy as they were six or seven years ago, George.'

'That's why I'm here. My little consortium is anxious to press on without too much hassle. You get me? We have to commit ourselves to the basics right now – supplementary services, the whole bloody blueprint from this edge to that edge way down there. We can't arse about for ever. You know what I have in mind, Tony?'

'No.'

'Whole new world down there nowadays, isn't there? Around Tower Bridge, I mean. And I want to keep up the momentum. A big development. Four office towers, another hotel, extended mooring facilities ... a river-bus terminal, maybe, and some restaurants that will make this little nosh-bar....' He looked about him and waved a disparaging hand.

'Your consortium?' said Webb dubiously.

'I love the way you say that, Tony, boy. Such diction! I've got a few more like you in tow. All villains, but Eton accents sticking out of their buttonholes. And not one of 'em minds if the money is mainly Arab. The meetings we've had, Tony, boy – and me and my Mr Monroe the only males not wearing dresses.' There was another pause as the avocado dishes were removed and clean plates brought in a flurry of warm napkins. 'Such a pity,' said Payne eventually, 'that the money has to come from abroad. That's something I'd like to discuss with you. If we play it clever, I might even get the Queen's Award for Industry.'

Across the restaurant Webb saw a middle-aged man in an alcove with a blonde at least fifteen years his junior. She was smiling dutifully into his face – even affectionately, if you wanted to interpret it that way – and at one stage stretched out a long, sleek leg. Webb absurdly wanted to go and warn them both – warn them about crazy joy, and

the stickiness and despondency that came afterwards ...
and in the end the outright terror.

He said: 'George, I don't know I'm the right chap to
approach. I'm in a very different position nowadays.'

'Quite so. Where you can exert a lot more leverage.'

'It's not like that.'

'It's going to have to be,' said George Payne very quietly.
'I want some names. Names of someone likely to let a lot
of waste paper go astray, like it did last time. Call themselves conservationists – all right, let 'em collect the waste
paper and recycle it.'

'Things are a whole lot twitchier now. You have no idea.
There's all this fuss about lobbying, and tie-ups with public
relations companies, and undeclared interests, and sources
of money that might be embarrassing, and –'

'Sources like your own?'

There was a sputtering and sizzling of Steak Diane, and
an attentive waiter with a dish of vegetables, and the aroma
of food appealing to George Payne but not, apparently, to
his companion.

'You always told me *those* sources couldn't be traced,'
said Webb apprehensively.

'Of course they can't,' said Payne, 'unless Mr Monroe
or myself told someone how to trace them.'

'But you wouldn't have any reason for doing that.'

'I knew that's how you'd see it, Tony.' Payne reached
across the table to bestow an avuncular pat on the wrist.
'Of course we wouldn't want to have any reason for doing
that. Or for mentioning any other little misfortune in the
past.'

5 DS John Miller had listened spellbound to the interview with the dejected Khalid Khan: listened through the interview room's bugs, and watched through the one-way mirror. The hastily summoned solicitor must have had a shrewd idea that the conversation was being monitored. He could have had no idea, though, just what his client was likely to come out with, which made his voice spiky and domineering, ready to talk down anything that was best left unspoken.

'My name's Nigel Coren. I'm your solicitor.'

Khan nodded submissively.

'When they charge you,' Cohen emphasized, 'whatever they do to you, you say nothing. However they intimidate you, not a single word. Got it?'

'They did not even search suitcases.' It was a plaintive, genuinely aggrieved feeling of injury. 'Just stopped me. They *knew*. How could they know?'

'I can't help you on that. All I can say is that we'll do all we can for you and your family. Your wife will be flown to London as soon as possible. I'll get word to her at the Georges Cinq.'

'She is not at Georges Cinq.'

Miller leaned forward. Coren's reaction plucked at his attention – a sudden tenseness across the shoulders, a sudden pallor in that podgy, self-satisfied face. Salter of Drug Squad raised an enquiring eyebrow but did not let himself be distracted from the framed picture of the two men and the edgy exchange of their voices.

'Where is she?' Coren sounded calm, but was fiddling with one gold cufflink.

'We did not stay at Hotel Georges Cinq.'

'Why not?'

'My wife is peasant girl. She was too nervous to stay in

64

such grand-looking place.' Khan raised his hands placatingly. 'I could not convince her.'

'Where *did* you stay?'

'Where we stay first time in Paris – Hotel Consort Invalides.'

'Hotel Consort. . .? You stayed there?'

Khan's timid smile, tinged with affection at the memory of his shy wife, faded into perplexity. 'Yes, sir.'

'Jesus.' It was quiet, but not too quiet to be picked up and relayed to the neighbouring room. Coren paused, then said stiffly: 'Don't make a statement of any sort to these people. I'll be back.'

He got to his feet, trying to look casual and businesslike. All in a day's work. Miller allowed time for the solicitor to reach the end of the corridor, then moved fast, leaving the bewildered Khalid Khan to the mercies of Salter.

A Bentley was drawing away from the Customs and Excise building as he emerged. Miller slid into the driver's seat of the Sierra and nosed his way into the traffic leaving Heathrow. It was tricky keeping Coren in sight, but would have been a lot trickier if the man hadn't sported such a conspicuous vehicle. They were two cars apart when they turned east on the M4. After a mile Miller overtook Coren, without glancing sideways, but another mile further on let himself drop back behind the concealment of a large luxury coach. From there on somebody else settled on Coren's tail – purely by chance, from all he could see. Very obliging of the bloke, whoever he was: a useful distraction.

At Hammersmith flyover Coren and Miller filtered out in turn towards the Broadway and up Shepherd's Bush Road. Coren made a swift turn into Brook Green, taking advantage of an elderly couple holding up the main road traffic by the zebra crossing. Miller had to wait a good ten fuming seconds before he could swerve across in pursuit. The Bentley was still conspicuous, slotted now into a parking space while Coren fed coins into the meter.

Miller slowed, wondering which way Coren was going

to walk off. For a moment he vanished down one of the side roads. Miller risked dawdling past the end of it; and had allowed himself just enough room to do a tight left turn in pursuit of the taxi that Coren had hailed.

It led him to the London Embassy Hotel.

Miller made sure Coren was well and truly inside, coasted to the end of the street and back again, and edged into a vacant space at the farthest extremity of the fore-court. He reached for the handset.

After half a minute the metallic voice was saying: 'I have car-to-car DS Collis, Channel 10.' And then Jim Collis: 'Right, what is it, John?'

'Where are you?'

'Stationary. Victoria Street, two minutes from the old homestead.'

'Time to get yourself un-stationary. But first of all wind down the window and drop your hot dog –'

'Who says I've got a –'

'Drop your hot dog *tidily* in the gutter,' said Miller. 'Then get here fast. London Embassy Hotel, Hammersmith.'

'On my way.'

Miller settled himself down. Days and nights of doing this sort of surveillance had taught him the position least likely to give him cramp after fifteen minutes or half an hour. It was not much use trying to make a quick getaway in the Sierra if your right leg had gone dead.

Collis made good time through whatever traffic was about, probably managing to scare a gratifying number of other drivers en route. His Cavalier came up the slip road to the forecourt and nudged up behind the Sierra's rear bumpers. He came round and sat beside Miller.

'What's here?'

'That brief from Heathrow. Nigel Coren. Been seeing Khalid Khan, and made a fast exit. Something Khan said.'

'Hm.'

There was a disturbing lack of interest in Jim Collis's

response. His eyes looked almost hooded. He was staring down between his knees, not at the floor or his shoes but at something which nobody else could see – something which had nothing to do with that bright hotel foyer or Coren or anyone else.

Miller said: 'Not still giving yourself indigestion with remorse? Or is it just the hot dog?'

'I saw the commander,' said Collis dully. 'Dragged me all that way back just to give me a rollicking.'

'Just to work off his frustration. Shouldn't take it to heart.'

'I think I'm for the boot.'

'Out? Out of Squad?'

'You can say that easily enough.'

'I'm not saying anything. I'm asking you.'

'Unless there's some divine intervention, I think I go.'

Miller did not take his eyes off the hotel entrance. 'So we get stuck in here,' he said gently. 'We hand them a big one and get pats on the head. But it's got to be a big one – big result.'

'But simplistic. Not to say patronising.' Anger surged in a drunken flush into Collis's cheeks, 'You know, that man in hospital isn't an easy situation for me to live with. . . .'

It had gone on for far too long. Every man on the beat or in plain clothes, any office or any division, got himself lumbered with a run of bad luck every now and then. One mistake or misfortune, and somehow there was another one waiting for you round the corner. Troubles never came singly. The bad patch had to be fought through, hoping you'd come out the other side and one day be able to look back and laugh at it all.

Collis found none of it a laughing matter.

Firstly there had been that squad mobile he had managed to wreck. It had been one hell of a chase through twisting back streets, and he had been dead unlucky to meet up with a large old Victorian cast-iron bollard which his quarry had cunningly led him towards. Just one of those things, which, unhappily, had cost one thousand eight hundred to repair – which Commander Cannock, for all his quietly wry humour, had shown himself unlikely to forgive or forget. Nor had the commander been much impressed by a hasty report which Collis had written out on the Littrick affair. It couldn't have been anything else but hasty: he was rushing to get it out of the way while still sweating despair over the outcome of that incident when he had hit a black man with a wrench.

All right, so the rampaging six-footer had himself been wielding a four-foot long iron bar. Against that a small wrench was not much of a defensive weapon, let alone an offensive one. There was a garden shed on fire, there were three large lunatics having the biggest punch-up you ever saw, and a kid nursing a fractured skull in the gutter – and lashing out with the wrench against that monster with the iron bar was the only thing to do. Now the man was still in hospital, still unconscious, still unresponding. That was going to make wonderful publicity for Scotland Yard: a Serious Crimes officer concusses and probably, in the long run, kills a black citizen. The iron bar would figure less prominently in the newspaper stories than the figure of a racist detective with his lethal wrench.

Collis had gone along to Westminster Hospital before coming on duty today. He had been told not to go, but some hopeless longing drew him there. He wanted to be on the spot when the good news came through: wanted to squeeze it out of the place with his bare hands.

Looking in through the window of the cubicle, he had seen his victim lying there motionless, his head bandaged and his arms and nose linked up in a cat's-cradle of wires.

A doctor coming out of a side corridor looked Collis up and down, impressed neither by his unbuttoned brown raincoat nor his helmet of black hair. 'I'm sorry, no visitors are allowed in the Intensive Care Unit.'

Collis reached for his ID. The doctor shrugged and

walked on, obviously thinking the detective sergeant must be on special guard duty.

Collis said: 'Look, can you help me?'

'Help you, officer?'

'Any change in the condition of that patient in there?'

The doctor turned and flipped through the charts hanging from the door handle. 'Stabilized position over the last twelve hours,' he said matter-of-factly.

'Is that good or bad?'

'Neither. He continues in coma.'

'What would you say was the outlook?' Collis persevered wretchedly.

'Not good. Savage attack. Are you supposed to be protecting this patient? A bit late for that. You'd be better off out there finding the man who did this to him.'

Collis said: 'I did it to him.'

The doctor looked even less impressed than before, and went on his way.

It was in no good mood that Collis had reached the Yard in answer to the commander's summons. Nor was the commander in a good mood. He made it briskly clear that there was a groundswell of opinion among certain ranking officers that rather than a rehabilitating 'shape up' it might be 'ship out' time for DS Collis. Commander Cannock observed with bleak tolerance that he was not entirely convinced of this: Collis's heart was in the right place, but he did keep tripping over his fists and his feet. Not to mention treating official vehicles like dodgem cars. Putting it crudely – which was something the commander rarely allowed himself to do – it was time Collis got his act together, tidied up his life a bit, and learned to discipline some of his more erratic tendencies.

The black man was not referred to. Until he came round and a proper testimony was taken, it would be incorrect to do so. And incorrect for Collis to go visiting. All of it unsaid: but the heavy shadow was there, nagging and accusing.

John Miller said: 'Jim, I think I'm going to have to stick close by you.'

'Don't force yourself. Bad luck has a habit of rubbing off.'

They found it easier to keep things flip and needle each other than to make outright declarations of friendship and co-operation. But Miller went on steadily: 'You need some important results, you clumsy sod, to improve your position. Here's a possible. So let's get to it. Okay?'

Collis nodded, but his gloom did not lift. 'What's the SP?'

This was a whole lot easier to talk about. 'Our chum Khalid Khan was supposed to go to one hotel in Paris, but from what we heard he stayed at another. Now why that should matter, I've no idea. But our friend in there' – he stabbed a thumb at the hotel foyer – 'got into a right tizzy when he heard it. God knows why.'

'And you're waiting for him to stroll out and tell you?'

'We're waiting,' said Miller, 'to find out why it was *here* that he came. Came right away, like a homing pigeon. Only it's not *his* home. So whose is it?' He wished the whole frontage of the hotel could be transparent, and every inside wall, so that he could look in and see Coren meeting somebody, drinking with somebody, reporting to somebody. They needed a face. He said: 'Did you replace the film in the camera?'

Without a word Collis opened the glove compartment and pulled out the Pentax. As Miller took it from him a grey Mercedes slowed past them and stopped at the foot of the hotel steps.

Coren was all at once there at the top, waiting.

'Coren,' murmured Miller, 'and . . . who?'

He raised the camera and fired off half-a-dozen shots as two men left the Merc and mounted the steps towards Coren. One of them was a heavy of some considerable weight, bulging out of his suit. The other's clothes had obviously been tailored for him, adding an air of expensive respectability to what was already a fair aura of self-confidence.

A car cut across Miller's sightline. It was an Astra, disgorging a man who chased the others up the steps and caught up with the bulkier one. He handed over a small package, seemed to be asking for a favour, something very immediate; and then was brushed aside, and hurried back to his Astra as if scared of being accosted by the doorman or a traffic warden.

Miller shot off half a dozen more pictures on his roll, while Collis studied the scene and tried to make some educated guesses about the story that held it all together. He came to the conclusion that his education had been sadly neglected.

As the Astra drew away and no longer obscured the view, they could see a group of men converging within the lobby. Coren and the more imposing of the newcomers were at once deep in conversation, until another man appeared at Coren's elbow. Even from this distance Miller could see, in dramatic dumb show, how Coren and his companion cringed and turned respectfully.

Miller tried a few more speculative shots before reaching for the R/T and putting in a DVLC on the Mercedes. He did not have to wait long for a reply. It was duly, correctly registered, no problem, and belonged to an accountant called David Monroe. That did not help a lot at the moment, but there might be some useful connection later. Let the fourth floor have a go at it.

The fourth floor in fact came reaching out within a matter of minutes. 'Message to DS Miller. Contact Commander Cannock immediately.' Collis winced at the sound of the name. 'Use land line.'

'Message understood. Four-four out.'

Miller replaced the handset and eased himself out of the car. There was a telephone kiosk at the far corner of the street.

Cannock, answering the call, wasted no words. 'Miller, you got anyone with you?'

'DS Collis.'

'Oh. Well, where's this grey Merc you've been asking about?'

'Parked outside the London Embassy Hotel.'

'Anyone with it?'

'It arrived two up,' Miller explained. 'I've shot some 400. Twenty snaps. One of the passengers spoke to the lawyer I was following – Coren. Sort of pleased with himself. Could be an accountant all right. Would that be Monroe?' When there was no reply, he added: 'And there's somebody else in there. I don't know –'

'Do what I tell you, now.' The commander was slow and deliberate. 'You and Collis get your cars quietly away from there. Don't get spotted. Back to the fourth floor – and *you* come and see me.'

When Miller returned to the Sierra, Collis glanced at him in silent enquiry.

'Blanked me,' said Miller. 'But he sounded a bit steamed up. Maybe something to do with this relationship between Monroe and Coren. Wonder if they've been having a target surveillance of their own on Monroe, whoever he may be?'

'Without telling us?'

'We're not going to get their received wisdom,' said Miller dourly. 'Never let the right hand know what the left hand's doing.'

'Then let's be on our way. Time I was off watch.'

'Not yet. Commander says back to the fourth floor with you.'

'Going to sharpen his claws on me a bit more?' Collis groaned. 'Anyway, are they replacing us here?'

'I don't know what the hell they're doing.'

Collis slid out of the Sierra and went back to the Cavalier. Miller set off, keeping a wary eye in his mirror. He felt a strange mutual bond with Jim Collis, but that did not mean he was not apprehensive about Jim's driving. The last thing he wanted was a smash up the backside in full view of that hotel lobby.

6 It had never for a moment occurred to George Payne that Colin Ettrick would obligingly go away. Ettrick, like some other eyesores cluttering up the scenery, would need a sharp lesson or two.

The first thing he would have done after that meeting in the cinema was surely to run to his suppliers. Payne knew who they were and where they were. He knew also that Ettrick would pride himself on playing things clever: he would sidle up to Santangelo, or more likely Santangelo's sidekick Rafaello, and tell them that he had been offered a better deal. George Payne was ready to match any price the mafia boys could demand.

Of course there would be some clever little shyster to say that George Payne was out of line, past it, a has-been. Three years now the Santangelo lot had been delivering brown paper bags at their own price and on their own terms. Colin Ettrick would put on his big act of being loyal to the old arrangement . . . but was capable of hinting that he might well decide to go in with George Payne if a prettier pattern could be spread out in front of him.

And if Santangelo and his cronies thought along the lines George Payne guessed they'd be thinking, it would undoubtedly occur to them that they too could deal direct with Payne, and cut out Ettrick altogether.

Or maybe they would cling together a little while longer, hoping to blow George Payne's head off before he introduced some explosive factors whose shrapnel would injure the whole lot of them. Either way, Payne was not unduly perturbed. He already had his own motives, his own priorities. And there was no reason why business should not be combined with pleasure. Which was why he suggested accompanying Monroe to Ronnie Scott's when Monroe had drawn a bead on Dacre. The operative they favoured was known to enjoy jazz, and spent a lot of his time in clubs where the righteous stuff could be heard. It was about the only thing George Payne would admit to having in common with a small-time hoodlum. He enjoyed good jazz: not, for once, from any ulterior motive but just because he found it alternately soothing and stimulating, twitching the sciatic nerve in tempo down his left leg and helping to ease the worries of running his extensive empire.

Payne and Monroe were sitting together when, halfway through a rhapsodic version of *Sweet Lorraine*, Hanley came in and crossed the room in search of an empty table. He did not risk even a knowing glance at the two of them, but sat close enough for Payne to observe exactly what was going on.

It took the last chorus and a two-bar coda before a man moved away from the back bar and sauntered towards the table.

Jeff Dacre was on the small side, inconspicuous, but fit and wiry. Not a man you would notice if you had not been tipped off about him: ferrety with his sharp little eyes but what on the whole you would describe as anonymous, if you described him at all. The unobtrusiveness was a big asset in his profession: he was an accomplished killer.

Hanley grinned a no-nonsense welcome. 'How's the finance, Jeff, lad? Still keeping it mainly in gilts?'

Dacre watched the group swinging subtly away, sad about having his concentration broken. The trombone slid into a solo rich with arabesques and sudden snarling attacks which faded submissively into half sweet, half sour meditation.

'Still on the game?' Hanley persevered.

Dacre turned his head away. The trombone slide swung invitingly towards the clarinet, and a throaty arpeggio led into another chorus.

In the subdued light Dacre was such a nonentity that anyone who bothered even to spare him a glance would wonder how long he would have to be shaken before waking up. Only the tautness of his bony fingers on the table hinted at his readiness to listen and respond. Jeff Dacre was a cool-headed, cold-hearted hit-man who had always taken a professional pride in his work without ever being stupid enough to boast about it. Among his more skilful accomplishments had been the mopping-up after a Libyan terrorist group had made a hash of a political killing outside a Kensington restaurant, creating derision rather than terror. Dacre was hired to settle the score tidily and efficiently – with a smooth skill which baffled Special Branch and restored the good reputation of his employers. Less than a month later he had removed two of the would-be assassins who had bungled the job in the first place.

And there had been that super-grass down in Essex who was putting on a big act as a gentleman farmer on his newly acquired estate, an act cut short when he shot himself while out shooting with the gentry. A sad accident, everyone had agreed; except for a few who did not agree but could never find any justification for their uneasiness.

Now Hanley repeated it: 'Still on the game?'

The number finished. The audience applauded. There was a minor reshuffle on the bandstand.

'Depends.' Dacre blinked out of his trance.

'On what?'

'Depends on the mark.'

'Friend of a mutual friend. Ettrick.'

'Colin Ettrick?'

'The same.'

'You want Colin Ettrick –'

'A *friend* of his.'

'Killed?' said Dacre mildly, philosophically.

'That's the prospect. It's the *cosa nostra*.'

Dacre nodded his head in an offbeat rhythm of his own. The prospect seemed to please him. 'Yes, I heard Ettrick was running with the mafia these days.'

'We'd like him to run with one less of them. They're

here on a boat. Only going to be around a few days, so we need some action.'

'How much you offering?'

'How much you asking?'

'Not a lot. Twenty grand would cover it.'

Hanley did not even glance across or lean across to get confirmation from Payne and Monroe. He said: 'You got it.'

'And a Walther P-38 or a Dan Wesson 357 Magnum, with twelve-inch barrel.'

Hanley's face creased into one of the more evil of his grins. 'I thought you'd say that. We got a Dan Wesson all nicely lined up for you. And five grand up, cash.' He shoved a piece of card casually across the table. It was his ticket from the hat check girl at the entrance.

Dacre picked it up just casually. 'When d'you want it?'

'Any time. At your convenience, really. I mean, I've told you the boat's only here a few days, but don't let it interfere with your social life or anything.' Hanley grew aggressive, but was drowned out by a sudden blasting chorus of the blues. 'I mean' – he shoved his head forward to make himself heard – 'it's only a sodding assassination.'

Not a muscle twitched in Dacre's cramped little face. 'Name of the target? The boat? Address?'

'Everything's with the money.'

'Is the geezer there right now?'

'Could be. Might be.'

'I'll go and look it over.' Dacre got up, yawning but with a wistful glance in the direction of the band. 'Meet me Eastlake Road, the end against the wall of Clapham Junction yards. Nine o'clock tomorrow night. With the rest of the money.'

Payne watched him go. After five minutes he beckoned Hanley to join Monroe and himself at their table. 'You reckon he's reliable?'

'We used him on that motorway contract while you were out of the country. That balls-up you wanted sorted out.

Ever get any comebacks?' asked Hanley with weighty pride. 'Ever read about it in your foreign papers – or even the English ones?'

'Not the airmail editions,' Payne conceded.

'In *any* of them? Anywhere?'

'Not a word.'

'That's it, then. He'll do it. Tonight, if the ravioli's around. Or early tomorrow morning. He's set on getting the rest of the money by the evening.'

'Which brings us to tomorrow.'

Monroe darted an expectant look from his boss to Hanley and back again. A little globule of saliva shimmered on the corner of his lip.

'Handing over the money,' he said, probing.

'We'll have fifteen thousand ready for Dacre when he calls to say the job's finished.' Payne, like Dacre, was more interested in the music than in what he was saying. He sounded faraway as he concluded: 'But Hanley might prefer to have that fifteen thousand when *he's* rounded off the job.'

Hanley looked pleased. 'High velocity rifle, this time?'

'All round better for security,' Monroe agreed.

'And the money –'

'After a result,' said Payne, even more distantly.

Miller had been sitting, in a growing miasma of boredom, watching the comings and goings in the lobby of the London Embassy Hotel earlier that night when the movement of one particular man jolted him out of his somnolence. A burly man, one of those Coren had approached earlier, was on his way out with a brief-case, hailing a taxi.

Slowly pulling away, Miller said into the R/T: 'Central four-four.'

'Receiving you, central four-four.'

'Report direct to commander. On the move with

unidentified member of group our lawyer addressed in hotel foyer as reported. Over.'

'Message understood, central four-four. MP out.'

Miller concentrated on the taxi ahead.

It had led him to Ronnie Scott's. He had seen the way his quarry studiously avoided speaking to someone else who had been in that original group – Monroe, no less, in a shadowy corner with a man whose face was shielded by Monroe's head and shoulders. Miller tried to get a glimpse of this other man's features, but did not dare to push forward into the room too conspicuously. In any case, he had a hunch it would be more productive to stay close to the entrance and the cloak-room where that brief-case had been deposited. The brief-case could be the key to the whole incident: a consignment of drugs for some important contact, maybe?

He was close enough to observe that apparently innocuous exchange of the cloakroom ticket for the case: innocuous if he had not already seen that ticket being passed across the table in the club.

On his way again, this time he found himself following a Ford Transit heading eastwards.

The R/T abruptly began demanding an account of his movements, and who and what he was tailing. Was he still following the man from the hotel? When he explained in detail, there was a pause as if Haldane, and behind him the commander, were trying by telepathy to figure out whether he had chosen the right one or was letting the bigger fish get away with something more important.

He reported arrival at Millwall Docks and the position of the van, weaving between towers of containers until it parked under cover close to a vessel whose name he could just make out: the *Filippo Lippi*. An Italian ship, registered in Napoli. Drugs: what else could it be?

'Target going aboard?'

Tucked under the shadow of a warehouse, Miller watched. The man was getting out of the Transit but was in no apparent hurry to step out into the lighted area of the quay or climb the gangplank. 'No,' reported Miller in an undertone. 'Seems to be sizing the place up. Biding his time.'

If it was a prearranged meeting, the other party was a long time in arriving to collect whatever might be in that case.

Maybe someone was going to saunter down the gangplank, nod a greeting, and simply collect the case. With heroin or cocaine in it? More likely the other way round: money in it, taken aboard and replaced with the required goods, brought back down again. As simple and barefaced as that. Not a Customs officer in sight; not a dockyard policeman.

In which case, when that little consignment came back down ...

In the first pale light of dawn, with the tall lights weakening under the opalescence of the sky, there was a faint tap on Miller's window. He jumped, his heart pounding, his legs tensing to thrust him out on the attack.

Collis grinned in, exaggeratedly pressing a warning finger to his lips. When Miller wound the window down he whispered: 'I've been sent to relieve you.'

'Like hell. I'm sitting this one out.'

'Go and curl up in bed like a good little –'

'I want to know what it's all about.'

'So does everybody back there.' Collis went round the back of the Sierra and got in beside Miller. 'No big handover – nothing to bring the Customs boys running in with the sniffer dogs?'

'Nothing.'

'Off you go. Leave me to it.'

'I wouldn't trust you on your own. Remember what we agreed.'

Collis shrugged and settled back into his seat. He did not crackle as he did so: he must have forgotten to pick up his breakfast breadsticks on the way.

They sat motionless until streamers of brightness suffused the sky, and in the distance there was a pulse of awakening traffic. A ship's siren groaned over the roof-tops.

'And who might this be?'

A Daimler had appeared at the north-western end of the dock area and was heading smoothly along the quayside towards the *Filippo Lippi*. It passed the corner where the Transit was waiting. The engine of the van started, and it nosed cautiously out and swung at an angle to intersect the path of the Daimler nearer the ship. In the still morning air it was all cool and unhurried, as if nobody was quite awake yet.

Miller drove the Sierra out from under cover, matching the pace of the others but holding well back.

The Daimler stopped at the foot of the gangplank. Three swarthy men got out, two in their mid-thirties, one older and more imperious. The two fell back to let the third go well ahead of them up the gangplank. As he reached the halfway mark, the Transit accelerated and came screeching on, skidding to a halt beside the Daimler.

The driver was leaning out of his open window. He yelled, 'Santangelo!'

Three heads turned. Now the older man instinctively gripped the rail and began to run upwards into the ship.

Four shots pumped into Santangelo's back. He froze for a moment, suspended at a crazy tilt on the gangplank; then toppled slowly sideways, and crumpled. Again the Transit screeched, its tyres rasping for a second before spinning and racing towards the far end of the dock.

'Round the back,' howled Collis. 'Cut him off.'

Miller needed no telling. He swung the wheel and wrenched the Sierra round on to a narrow slip road.

Collis was reaching for the handset. 'Central four-four. Shooting Millwall Docks. In pursuit of suspect. Ambulance urgently required *Filippo Lippi*.'

Out on the main road they could see the brake lights of

the Transit far ahead as it slowed and then vanished round a corner. Miller put his foot down and began to close in.

The R/T came back at them. 'Ambulance on its way. What shooting? And where's your suspect?'

'In sight. Heading on to the East India Dock Road, turning back west.'

'He's still armed?'

'Didn't see him throw the gun away.'

'Then hold back.'

'There's two of us,' said Collis tensely. 'We'll find a way of –'

'You'll hold back.' It was the familiar pessimistic growl of DI Mackie. 'In the first place we don't want a shoot-up. And in the second place, if what Miller reported earlier fits what the commander's thinking, this is the one who could lead us to the bigger ones. Tail him all the way home. And let us know just where that is. We'll have him covered every minute from now on.'

'Understood, guv.'

'And don't lose him.'

Miller had no intention of losing him. Morning traffic was beginning to make things tricky, but when the killer finally parked on a patch of waste ground in an otherwise trim Shoreditch back street, the Sierra was able to make a leisurely detour round the far side of the exposed area without once losing sight of the man. He went into a house in a recently repainted terrace. Collis sauntered unobtrusively to the end of the road, checked its name, checked the number of the house, and came back to report in.

'Nice work,' said Mackie with uncharacteristic generosity. 'Just keep that place under surveillance until I get a relief round to you.'

Miller said: 'We'd rather see this through, guv, now we're here.'

'And fall sound asleep?' It was DCI Haldane this time, grim and brooking no argument. 'You'll come off duty when you're told to come off. Go and get yourself some breakfast and bed. We may need you very wide awake by this evening.'

They waited for their replacements without uttering a word. Neither of them wanted to relinquish any part of this operation. There was a prickly feeling of being so close to the truth: close enough to crack it, if only they could burst into that house over the way, grab that hoodlum, and beat every last little detail out of him.

Instead of which they were relieved, Collis went off to retrieve his squad car and book it back in, and Miller went off to pick up his own Peugeot. He was not wasting time on breakfast and bed. An hour or two's kip in the mid-afternoon maybe. Right now he had a date to keep: one that he had had to postpone twice already because of the demands of the job. Postponements like that had led to a lot of the trouble in the past.

Colonel Railton met him at the gates and accepted a lift for the few hundred yards down the curving drive. He said something flippant about his age, and his gammy leg; but then was silent, sensing that his son-in-law was in no mood for even the most well-meaning conversational trifles.

John Miller felt a constriction across his chest. He was gnawed by fright. It was only a child he was going to see, still little more than a baby, but he was more scared than if he had been pacing towards a killer with a gun in his hand. Everything about this hurt.

'She's been away again?' he said as the Peugeot approached the house that had once been so warm and welcoming. It had seen better days – the upkeep was proving more and more of a strain on Railton – but it had meant so much to him. And to Vanessa, who couldn't even be bothered to visit it most of the time nowadays.

'Away again, yes,' said Railton sadly.

'Another four weeks ski-ing?'

'Away,' Railton repeated. 'But she's back in London now. Ready for the court hearing.'

They got out of the car. Miller was about to head for the porch, but his father-in-law touched his arm and pointed through the windbreak of bushes to the wide, gently sloping lawn beyond.

He had memories of that lawn, too. Vanessa had been a ravishing, radiant sight on her father's arm in the little Buckinghamshire village church down the road. And she had seemed even more beautiful at the reception on the lawn, with the sunshine and clear skies benevolently smiling down on the bride and groom.

Now there was another sight that ought to have been as flawlessly joyful as those earlier ones: where the lawn levelled out above the lake, his two-year-old daughter sat engrossed in some game with the nanny Railton had engaged for her.

Miller's feet refused to carry him any further.

Railton said: 'There's something I want you to know. I've seen the lawyer again, and he's gone away to think up ways and means . . . some trust or other . . . to give little Abigail something. Something to help her, you know, independently of anything else, when I . . .' He shrugged, not finishing the sentence.

'You mustn't do too much,' said Miller awkwardly. 'I wouldn't want you to. . . .' Now he, too, could not finish a remark. 'I blame myself,' he snapped out. 'And the job.'

'You've got a fine career. And I know that you've done it all for her – for the three of you. She should have stayed and supported you.'

The pain was still clawing at Miller's chest. If only he could go back and find some other way of handling things, balancing up the job and his home life. Vanessa had been left alone too much; he had put in too much overtime, taken on too many responsibilities, fought his way too ambitiously up the ladder. But hadn't it been to provide her with the things he thought she deserved? If only. . . .

He began to walk down the slope towards Abigail. The new nanny turned and smiled uncertainly.

Behind him, Railton said: 'Her name's Bridie. Irish.'

Irish. Just like that bastard who had wormed his way into Vanessa's life. Abigail with an Irish nurse and Vanessa with an Irish fancy man.

He stood above them. 'I'm Abigail's father.'

Bridie scrambled up to her feet and held out her hand. Then she looked down, and put out the other hand to Abigail.

'Abigail, it's your daddy.'

The smile and the turn of that blonde head were so much like Vanessa's that Miller was choked, paralysed again. Suddenly he stopped and swept Abigail up in his arms, and she squealed with delight, and kissed his cheek and nuzzled into his shoulder, and laughed – not at anything special, but just with sheer childish happiness. Miller clutched her even more tightly, and she went on laughing into his ear as he paced around the edge of the lake. He was sick with love for this tiny, warm, adoring and adorable creature. There was no way – couldn't, in this world, be a way – that anyone could simply carry her off like a piece of dispossessed furniture.

Yet, as they came to a halt on the far side of the lake and looked across it at Railton, who was waving slowly so that Abigail could see him and wave back, the awful truth came seething up to poison his throat and his mind. Vanessa was not so wrong, damn her. That lust to see a job through to the finish, no matter what the danger and what the hours, had been his downfall: the erosion of their marriage. Even with all these pangs doing awful thngs to his chest and his stomach, wasn't he already halfway along the road back to that baffling, infuriating business of the men in the London Embassy Hotel and the stooges walking into the trap at Heathrow and the man in the Ford Transit who had been paid – oh yes, he had been paid all right – to shoot down an Italian delivering some sort of cargo at Millwall Docks?

Obsessions like this had lost him his wife and threatened

his daughter. But he could not slacken his grip.

He wanted to *know*.

The Transit sat in shadow between two feeble street lamps, with a haze of railway marshalling yard lights touching the high walls with a sulphurous dust. The driver looked along a cement roadway into the yards over a sunken track, abstractedly watching a couple of late commuter trains rushing through. Goods wagons clanked and grated away to his left.

To his right, by a crossroads under a warehouse festooned with scaffolding, Miller and Collis sat watching Dacre. They knew by now that his name was Dacre. The address had been checked, the background swiftly summarized. An ex-musician, reputedly quite good on the trumpet until somebody pushed his teeth in. There had been one vicious GBH – acquitted on insufficient evidence three, four years back. Nasty, but not easy to pin down.

A metallic voice between Miller and Collis said: 'MP, MP to central four-four.'

'Central four-four receiving. Buggerall to report. On the ten-minute mark, no move since he made a phone call. Very quiet. It stinks. Suggest he's waiting upcoming rendez-vous.'

'Message from Mr Haldane. He's sending you two sharpshooters from D11. With you in forty, forty-five minutes.'

Miller grunted. His inside still felt bilious, and his reactions were becoming acid as well. Whatever was going on, it would surely be over within twenty or thirty minutes at the outside. This Dacre character was not the type to sit studying the trains going by for an entire evening.

On the same mental wavelength as Miller, Collis stressed into the handset: 'We have one hand gun. Over and out.'

They resumed their remote contemplation of the dark head just visible in the cab of the Transit.

'Come up with anything brighter than him having done

the job and come here for the pay-off?' asked Miller.

'What else?'

'We've got to cover all the angles.'

But he knew, and Collis knew in his bones, that this was the scenario that read right. Dacre had killed the mark, driven here and parked his motor, telephoned, and now was waiting for his fee. They knew he had a hand gun: after what had happened by the *Filippo Lippi*, they knew what result he was capable of getting with it.

Just supposing that the paymaster, when he came, had a shotgun?

High time that their own sharpshooters put in an appearance.

They saw Dacre lean forward. From this angle there was nothing else to be seen for a moment, then it came into view: a BMW on one of the cement tracks across the marshalling yard making its way to a junction with the road under Dacre's bonnet. It was like watching a jumbo jet coming slowly off the runway along a spur towards its appointed place. But before reaching the junction the BMW stopped and flashed its headlights twice. Dacre responded and, after a moment's deliberation, got out of the Transit.

He waved the BMW to come closer.

It stayed where it was.

The quickest way to reach it was across two converging railway tracks. Dacre waited for a goods train to clatter past; hesitated again; stepped warily over the lines. It was only as he passed under a light that Miller noted there were binoculars slung round his neck. Once again he paused, and this time studied the BMW through the glasses. What he saw seemed to satisfy him, for he went on his way.

'Time to get a bit closer to the action,' said Miller.

The two of them left the Sierra and clung to the wall of the yards until there was nothing for it but to strike out across the open tracks. Fortunately several trucks on a siding masked their movements to within twenty or thirty yards of the BMW.

The car's engine was still ticking over. Leaning on a coupling between two trucks, Miller could see it begin to back away, reversing smoothly into a huddle of sheds with a bank of signal-boxes rearing above them. He jerked his head at Collis. As one, they scuttled for the end of the siding, crouching round it into the cover of an abandoned hut. There was a heavy reek of diesel and something which could have been rotten fish.

'Hanley! Show yourself!' Dacre was alarmed by the stealthy withdrawal of the BMW. 'This is as far as I go.'

Miller and Collis flattened themselves against the end of the signal-box block. Beyond it they could glimpse the BMW; and could see that there was now nobody in the driver's seat.

'Christ, where . . .?'

'Hanley, I want to see you. Come on – out here.'

Dacre had to skip to one side as a diesel shunter rolled past without the driver even noticing him.

'Hanley!'

Dacre was out in the open, very well illuminated, and he suddenly realized just how exposed he was. It was too late. From the far end of the range of signal-boxes came a single shot. It blew one side of Dacre's head away, but something kept him moving forward.

'Where'd it come from?' Miller stumbled out into the open, towards Dacre.

Another shot hit Dacre. He bent forward, hitched his right leg agonizingly along, and began to sag.

'Where's it coming from?' asked Collis desperately.

'Up!' Miller gestured upwards at the signal-box roof. At the same time he began to run. There was another shot. He swayed to one side, clutching his arm. It had felt like a kick in the elbow. It was more than that.

Collis came out of cover like a battering-ram with a score of highly trained men carrying it. He saw that Miller, stopped in his tracks, was a wonderful target for anyone aiming for a bull's-eye. Smashing into him, he rolled both of them over the rails into a huddle on the hard pillow of a sleeper. Bullets whined around them.

His head well down, Miller rasped: 'Where is he?'

'Up aloft somewhere, like you said.'

'Take the gun.'

It was the only one they had between them. The re-inforcements were far too late in arriving. Collis hunched himself along until he heard and felt the rail resonating with the approach of a goods train. It was clanking down the line over which Miller, still winded, was lying. He turned back, forgetting caution and cover, and dragged Miller off the line. The train rattled past. Bullets rattled within inches.

Collis no longer had any idea of what might have happened to Dacre. He hadn't got much idea of what was likely to hit him or Miller next. But on his hands and knees he crawled towards the direction of that last fusillade of shots. He wasn't interested in correct procedure: let that bastard raise his head, and it would be blown off.

Miller tottered to his feet and made a run for the signal-boxes. Dust spurted up close to him. The flash came from sheds to the left. Miller went stubbornly on. Collis was heading for the spot where they had last seen Dacre. Another flash altered its direction, and there was the screech of a bullet across metal not eighteen inches from his head. But Dacre was visible now, sprawled below a tall arc lamp standard.

Dacre they had to have, if any of this was to be turned into any kind of sense.

'You – get down,' ordered Collis. 'Get flat!'

What was left of Dacre hauled itself half upright and reached for a gun.

'Police,' said Collis.

He rushed Dacre and grabbed the gun. But there would have been no strength in Dacre's dying finger to pull the trigger. They had lost him.

Miller, unarmed, was plodding on towards the complex of signal boxes. He was halfway up the outer staircase when the boxes began to blow apart. Pump-guns sent glass splinters out over the marshalling yards like a snowstorm. Collis made a dash, expecting to see nothing but a mangled mess cut to ribbons by the lethal ice particles.

Miller, hugging his arm but still ready to go, in whatever direction was needed, said: 'Not just Hanley, whoever Hanley is. Another two. That way.' His gesture made no sense whatsoever.

'You okay?'

'We've lost 'em. What about our friend out there?'

'Dead,' said Collis.

At last Miller collapsed, bent in on himself. 'We've done the complete works on this, haven't we?'

'Screwed it,' said Collis. 'Totally screwed it.'

7 The morning light on the marshalling yards was no more cheerful than the high, foggy lamps had been the night before. There were more signals at red than there had been during the night shunting hours: a whole section had been blocked off to allow uniformed policemen and a photo team to pick their way over the tracks and the slivers of shattered glass frm the signal-boxes, searching for cartridge cases and anything else that might be significant.

Detective Inspector Mackie pushed his right hand through his hair, stonier and greyer than usual in this bright but cold light. Nobody had picked up anything of value so far. And reports from the *Filippo Lippi* added up to nothing. It had all the makings of a *Mary Celeste*. Only two Asians and an Indian were left, all the Italian crew had gone, taking to their heels after last night's shooting, including the master, Captain Alberto Ceccio. Mackie headed for the end of the signal-boxes, where John Miller was leaning with one shirt sleeve rolled up, a tape dressing around his arm.

'Any pain?'

Miller shook his head. 'Only a flesh wound. A quarter inch deep.' He studied Mackie's wooden expression. 'Any more form on the deceased?'

'There's talk of him being a professional hit man, but nobody so far has enough facts to pin on the talk. Don't think we should waste much time on him, particularly as he's dead.'

Collis had come over to join them from the end of the search line. 'But there's got to be *some* arrests out of this. I mean, it's all tied up in some way with that London Embassy Hotel lot.'

'We're not all dead ignorant on the fourth floor. That

91

little matter hasn't escaped Mr Haldane's notice. Or the commander's.'

'Then why . . .? I mean, we've got six on Kodak. A few of those must be guests. I mean, I'm not shy. I'll walk in and nick 'em with pleasure,' said Collis fervently. 'So what's going on?'

That trigger-happy eagerness made Mackie's lips tighten into a line so thin as to be almost invisible. 'We're going back to the Yard. Maybe Mr Haldane will tell you.'

Detective Chief Inspector Haldane was waiting for them in the projection room on the fourth floor. He rubbed his eyes. It looked as if he had been watching too much flickering film and too many blown-up stills before the others got here.

There were two projectors. Side by side they showed the scene which had puzzled Costigan, of Monroe obsequious beside a well-dressed man who had just got out of a Daimler, and the picture Miller had taken of the two of them together in the hotel lobby.

'Same man?' said Haldane.

Miller nodded agreement. Collis said: 'Definitely Who?'

'That's the point. We don't know. But he has to be a big one. And you reckon he's staying at that hotel?'

'Check it in five seconds,' volunteered Collis. 'His description with the hall porter —'

'No. The head banger approach is what we don't want. We handle this like a delicate flower. We're going to go now and meet some senior policemen. They'll ask you some questions. Just answer them.'

The four of them walked to the lift, while the DCI continued: 'We have to know who this Mr Z is. The guy Monroe's talking to in your pictures and in C11's. We'll talk a bit more to C11. Right. How do you go about finding this man?'

'Usual procedures,' said Miller crisply. 'One: check with London Embassy Hotel security officer. All informal. Two: follow Mr Z whenever he shows his face, and see what ideas he triggers off. Three: hotel register name checked against Inland Revenue, DHSS, DVLC, passport office. Four: if this is all a blank draw, he's an out-of-town finger or latter-day finger. . . . Then go to HM prisons, turn over people of his age group. Before or after that, screw his hotel room.'

'Before,' Haldane ordered. 'And there's one missing from your list. Sergeant Collis . . .?'

'Can't imagine, guv.'

'Miller?'

'Thought that covered everything, guv.'

'In case he's a yachtsman, check Lloyd's Register.'

They reached their floor and headed down the corridor towards C11.

'They're going to chat to us,' explained Haldane, 'about David Monroe, accountant, nutter. Very dangerous. It's Monroe's deferential attitude to this man that's making us think we're on to a gent who's really big.'

'If he's very big,' said Collis, 'why only two of us? And why us two, sir?'

'We keep the faces down to a minimum. Otherwise it becomes Drug Squad, Customs, Robbery Squad, a mess. It only takes two to organize a trap: one to set it, one to keep the other alive.'

Haldane led the way into C11, where Costigan and half a dozen senior officers from their earlier meeting were assembled.

Superintendent Costigan wasted no time. 'Sit down, gentlemen. An informal chat. A few questions. I'll put mine up first if there are no objections.' It was quite clear that he anticipated no objections. 'Sergeant Miller, at Heathrow you followed a solicitor – Coren – after he'd interviewed an incoming passenger caught with five kilos of heroin.'

'Yes, sir.'

'Why did you take the initiative to follow him?'

'It's all in my report, sir. He reacted a little oddly to some information the arrested man gave him – to do with not staying in a particular Paris hotel. It seemed curious.'

'Are you sure that's the only reason you followed him, sergeant?'

'Why wouldn't it be, sir?'

'I'll ask the questions, sergeant.'

Another officer said placatingly: 'I think what the superintendent is asking you, sergeant, is whether any other police colleagues had been talking to you about this lawyer before you witnessed him and his upset at Heathrow? Meaning that this is an important investigation and we want to know if there's the slightest chance of any little leakages occurring.'

'It was my own initiative to follow this lawyer,' said Miller.

'Why did you photograph him, sergeant? Had you received any instructions to photograph anybody?'

'No, sir.'

'Is it your normal procedure,' intervened yet another of the group, 'to take snaps of irascible lawyers meeting unknown people?'

Miller's patience was wearing thin. 'There had been a suspicious reaction by a lawyer in the presence of a client who had been caught with a hefty consignment of heroin. There was a camera in my mobile. I used it.'

'I think we may be getting ahead of ourselves, gentlemen,' said Costigan. 'Let's go through Sergeant Miller's and Sergeant Collis's reports, from the top.'

They all had copies. As they began to read them through, Miller and Collis looked at each other and then at Haldane, bewildered. When heads rose from the final paragraphs of the reports, Haldane came to the rescue. Before Costigan or any of his colleagues could start up again, he briskly summed up the events of the last few hours, and then said: 'One of Sergeant Miller's suggestions is one which I recommend putting into action without delay. I want to see them on the move – fast.'

The lettering of the shop off Commercial Street proclaimed it as the National Security Company. It was a fine, resounding name for a one-man business run by a bright ex-lag whose seamed, cunning little face acquired a few more despairing wrinkles as he opened the door to Miller and Collis.

'Oh, no, this can't go on.'

They walked into the shop. It looked a far less successful enterprise than it actually was. There were only a few run-of-the-mill items like locks and burglar alarms on the shelves. All the good gear was kept under the counter.

Collis poked around behind a stack of unlabelled boxes. 'Doing all right, Denny? Saw you the other day – nice, that C-reg Merc.'

'You can't just wander in here and –'

'Kids all well? Six of them at private school by now, isn't it?'

'Two kids,' protested Denny Rogers.

'We want a borrow of – let's see, how does it go in your catalogue? – "bug, room, for the use of". Make it three.'

'Why can't you rent the thing like anybody else? I do rent to police forces, you know.'

'Yes, we know. Iranian police forces . . . Argentine police forces. . . . Right, then. Room bugs, the 10-watt, with two hand receivers. And don't bother with the gift wrapping.'

Rogers sighed wearily, and began to root behind some tangles of flex on a low shelf. He fished out a plain box and lifted the lid to reveal a neat array of bugs and receivers. 'I want them returned in good condition.'

'Within the week,' promised Miller. 'I'll see you get them back. And many thanks.'

'You could learn a thing from Mr Miller,' said Rogers meaningfully to Collis. 'At least he's got manners. He does say "thanks".'

'We all think he's one of nature's true gentlemen.'

The two of them left, and Miller drove in what was

becoming the all too familiar direction of the London Embassy Hotel. He parked a fair way down the road from the hotel entrance, and took the package of equipment off the back seat. They were strolling towards the hotel as two men came down the steps: two men in motion, not frozen into photographs as they had so recently seen them. One was Monroe, the other his still nameless friend, heading for a grey Mercedes.

'You go after them,' said Miller.

Collis turned on his heel and went back to the Sierra.

The hotel security officer, Harrington, had made preliminary enquiries from the description given over the phone. 'Must be a chap called Hanrahan,' he announced as soon as Miller entered his tiny office.

'That his real name?'

'That's how he's registered. No reason to suppose any different. Not so far, anyway.'

'He's just gone out.'

'You saw him?'

'Just as I was on my way in here.'

'Couldn't be better, then. But we'll take no chances.'

They went up in the lift to the third floor. Harrington opened the door of a linen cupboard and indicated that Miller should stay inside until they could be sure the coast was clear.

He walked three doors along and rang the bell of what he had already assured Miller was the largest and most expensive suite in the hotel. There was no reply. He tapped on the door; rapped more loudly; called 'Mr Hanrahan . . . security officer.'

When there was still no response he used his house key and went in.

'Sergeant Miller.'

Miller swiftly crossed the corridor and surveyed the luxury in which their mysterious friend liked to live. This was certainly no small-time operator.

'Don't tell me what you're going to do,' said Harrington.

'But whatever it is, let it not be too obvious.'

'Don't worry about that.'

'I'll leave you to it.'

Alone, Miller checked on the four interconnecting rooms, appraising the likely places where the man and his associates might sit and talk. In the end he installed one bug in a table lamp and another in the telephone before carrying out a fuller recce of the bathroom. There was more in his bag then Denny Rogers' equipment. He had come supplied with ten different brands of toothpaste. One of them, to his relief, matched the half-used tube in a mug above the washbasin. He put gloves on, gently picked up the tube and dropped it into a plastic specimen bag, then squeezed his new tube until it resembled the shape and contents of the older one. His third bug went into the shaver socket.

There had been no interruptions. When he left the suite he allowed himself an almost inperceptible nod to the watchful Harrington, and went out into the street at an unhurried pace.

He wondered how Jim Collis was making out.

Collis had not expected the Mercedes to lead him round Parliament Square and then come to a standstill beside the House of Commons. He dawdled, waiting to see who was going to get out and where he would be going.

Instead, a tall man with an authoritative bearing came towards the Mercedes. His confident manner seemed to desert him, though, as he drew closer, turning to the same sort of obsequiousness Monroe had shown this Mr Z. As the car door opened the tall man almost scuttled inside, head well down, as if not wishing to be identified. It was unusual for an MP to be so diffident.

In spite of the busy traffic the Mercedes set a spanking pace through the streets. It was all Collis could do to keep his target in sight. He found himself taking chances, cutting dangerous corners, grunting to himself with frustration and mounting impatience, stamping on the accelerator and then on the brakes, losing the Merc in the tangle and then finding it again. They were heading north – to a meeting, a restaurant, a rendezvous with some other important figure in the whole pattern?

The Mercedes turned off across Hampstead Heath. Collis thought of radio-ing in to report; narrowly missed a truck shooting out of a side lane, and thought better of it. One thing at a time.

That blasted truck had nipped in ahead of him. It completely obscured his view of the Merc. He tried to pull out and pass, but the truck was bouncing from one side to the other. Then it slowed, as if the driver was looking for something on the right-hand side of the road.

Collis swore, and made a wild dash to the left, beginning to pass on the inside. He was doing seventy, and still it might not be enough. There was only a narrow gap between the erratic truck and a line of parked cars.

He was going to make it.

Then one of the cars began to pull out. He caught a glimpse of a white head as the old dear, too busy concentrating on the mere business of driving and changing gear, came out without so much as glancing in her mirror. He braked violently and swung out behind the truck. At the same time the truck slowed. The Sierra jarred into it with an impact that shuddered up Collis's legs and spine and through his teeth.

The tailgate dropped and, before his very eyes, a pile of secondhand electrical goods started to shower on to his bonnet and the road. The Sierra was completely out of control, hitting a refrigerator and bounding off an electric cooker. Collis saw the road swing towards him at an absurd angle. He was belting straight across it, over the opposite kerb, and then ahead of him was an embankment leading down, forever down. The car came to rest with its nose against a tree stump, while fragments of a washing machine clanked and thudded down around it.

Somebody was shouting apoplectic abuse. Collis, clutching his neck and pushing himself out on the slope, saw what was presumably the driver of the truck tottering towards the edge of the embankment.

This time there was no argument about it: he had to radio in. It was not an agreeable experience.

Nor was the voice of DCI Haldane when he and Mackie reached the scene, hard behind a garage truck which set about winching the wrecked Sierra back up to the road.

'You could have killed a dozen people. If it had been anyone else who'd done this pathetic thing, I'd have said it was a moment of madness. But with you it's more than moments. It's all the bloody time.'

The truck driver was giving details to a uniformed policeman. Passers-by were looking in wonderment at the assortment of goods strewn along the pavement and down the grassy embankment.

'And where the hell,' Haldane raged on, 'is Miller?'

'I suppose he's still at the hotel, sir. Oh ... or somewhere.'

'Or *somewhere*?'

Haldane got back into the waiting Ford Granada. Mackie stood with one hand on the door, uncertain whether they were to take Collis along with them. Haldane's glare made it clear what the answer was: *Find your own way home.*

There was a sudden tingling snap, and the tortured whine of metal as the tow rope broke and the Sierra went back down the embankment again.

Collis stared despairingly at the havoc he had created.

8 The big coup was planned not just for itself alone, though the sheer flamboyance of it made George Payne's mouth water. In another, more detached part of his mind was the awareness that to counterbalance such self-indulgence he still needed more sober achievements – things achieved not by an extravagant head-on defiance of the law but by calculated, well-mannered bending of it. And the profits from the big assault would provide nice sums for investment: a healthy injection into Payne's property deals. Very respectable, property was. You could collect a knighthood or even a peerage if you screwed your rivals cunningly enough and shoved up enough buildings and stripped enough assets here and there.

Not that George Payne included such honours among his present aims. It would have been fun, just to prove how it could be done, but the pleasure would soon have worn off. He knew that much about himself. A bit of profitable respectability on the side as a property tycoon was one thing; permanent ennoblement was quite another.

He smiled across the restaurant table at Anthony Webb. Now, here was someone who could confidently expect a knighthood in the reasonably near future if he kept his nose clean. And he would enjoy every minute of it: much more than he was enjoying himself right at this minute.

Payne said: 'So you think those little loose ends can be tidied up, Tony?'

'I'm doing what I can. It's not a thing you can rush through overnight. I think I see a way to do it and keep everybody happy.'

'Just so long as you keep *us* happy.'

Webb managed a feeble grin.

'Right,' said Payne. 'Now to the next stage.'

The grin faded. 'The next stage? I thought that once we'd cleared this out of the way –'

'That's just it. It's simply clearing things out of the way. Once that's been done, we have to move on down that way. Now, has it ever occurred to you that there's a source of institutional money in this country no one's really exploited?'

'Which is?' said Webb cautiously.

'Politically committed funds.'

'Look, after all that trouble the unions had over shifting their assets to –'

'I'm talking about the Right, not the Left.'

'You'd better explain.'

'For starters, think of the docklands. Out go the Labour voters. Your people are working on that already in certain sectors, right? Condemn the poor housing, get a lot of kudos for facing up to it so boldly and, like I said, out go the Labour voters. Level the place, and in come the sunrise industries – upwardly mobile support residents.'

'Just a minute. You were talking about exploiting money. Exploiting it how?'

'Ought to appeal to your backers. Certain parts of London – black people, poor housing. Low cost acquisition. Don't tell me you don't know somebody who might be persuaded that rolling up units in these areas for scheduling blacks out, industry and the upwardly mobile in, has a certain . . . well, missionary value?'

Webb leaned furtively out of their alcove to see if anyone he knew had moved in on the neighbouring tables. The place was usefully, reliably out of the way; but still his nerves were on edge.

'Who would I know?' he asked.

'Sir Edward Deaseley,' said Payne. 'The Bonded Company. You agree?'

This time Webb's smile, though feeble, had a certain reluctant admiration in it. 'Oh, yes. I see what you mean.' He picked up his knife and fork. 'Very much to the right of Genghis Khan. Yes, I can see he'd very much like to politicize his money.'

'I wonder if anybody's ever put a proposition like this to him without frills.'

'Just what would the proposition be?'

'Buying Brixton.'

Webb stared. 'You're not serious. You don't simply go out and buy a whole borough.'

'Members of Parliament did it all the time in the old days, so I've been told.'

'You're not serious,' said Webb again.

'I'm completely serious. Start by buying up large chunks of it. For a place only seven or eight minutes from the Thames, housing and sites are cheap.' Payne leaned back expansively in his chair. 'It makes good sense. So I want you to arrange a get-together.'

'With Deaseley?'

'With Deaseley.'

'Could be a problem.'

'Why?'

'He's a personal friend of the Home Secretary. He wouldn't talk deals with you without running a check. He'll soon get access to police facilities. A lot of old deals might get raked over. You know, the messianic right and whited sepulchres and . . . no, it's a non-starter.'

Webb looked pleased with himself. So far as he was concerned, the matter had been effectively written off. He went on eating with renewed appetite.

Payne said quietly: 'I want to get it started.'

'George, your background isn't exactly what it might be. I wouldn't have thought you *wanted* too much digging and delving. Frankly, I doubt if you'd pass muster.'

'I'm not asking what you think or what you doubt, Tony.' It was even quieter. 'I want a meeting with Edward Deaseley.'

'I . . . I'll try.'

'You'll do better than that,' said Payne.

And then he turned his attention to another string which needed a warning tweak. Tony Webb took very little skill to manipulate. The Ettricks were going to need rather more. In their case it called for brawn as well as skill. The removal of Santangelo had been a clear warning, but Ettrick had not come back with any offer to renew negotiations. Give him a bit more time? Or give him a closer, more personal warning?

George Payne's tastes favoured the latter. Time was what he did not have a lot of.

Hanley was by no means exhausted by his handling of Jeff Dacre. Hanley, in fact, was well and truly steamed up and ready to carry on the good work. With the help of Denton and Ennis he would really enjoy this next little task.

The target was Colin Ettrick's younger brother, Johnny. Next time it might have to be Colin himself, but for the moment Johnny would serve as an example. Nobody could call George Payne an unreasonable man. He was still prepared to do business with the Ettrick mob so long as they acknowledged who was calling the tune from now on.

Payne tugged the string and set this particular little act in motion.

Johnny Ettrick was too brash, too sure of himself to consider that his beloved white Porsche would be tailed by a rival. The Ettricks had grown big-headed in the absence of serious competition. It was a big-headed Johnny who parked his expensive car outside the expensive French restaurant in Maida Vale and parked the blonde tart along with it.

'Take about a minute,' he said confidently. Hanley had drawn up no more than a hundred yards away without even attempting any concealment, but Johnny did not bother to look round. 'You sit here and work out how you're going to please me.'

The blonde twitched her head in what she must have thought was a roguish manner. 'Oh, Johnny.'

'Let your imagination run riot.'

She giggled again as he headed into the restaurant. Hanley nodded to Finch and Ennis, who got out and leaned on the wall. With Denton at his heels, Hanley himself sauntered towards the restaurant.

Inside, Johnny was saying: 'Right, what's it all about?'

The proprietor, whose name was inscribed above the entrance as Jean-Paul de Laubinque, stood for a moment in the doorway from the kitchen, then advanced fearfully into the restaurant. Johnny sat down, fished a bread roll from its basket, and chewed a mouthful, giving the man time to break out in a thin, oily sweat.

'M'sieur Ettrick, I have had a few troubles.'

'No, no, that won't do. We sorted out all your troubles, remember? That nasty bunch of Cypriots doing all that mischief, like terrorizing your customers and firebombing your *hors d'œuvres* ... no, those days are over. Aren't you grateful for all that protection?'

'M'sieur Ettrick, I make no complaint.'

'That arrangement we came to was quite generous, if you ask me. A little cash, and channelling your orders through my Northways Catering. No hassle, eh?'

Jean-Paul de Laubinque tried to explain something with a few graphic gestures of his hands and shoulders, but made no sense.

Hanley eased his way towards the bar and poured himself a drink. Laubinque glanced sideways at him. Ettrick paid no attention.

Johnny said: 'So what's gone wrong? No cash last week. No orders. So maybe you're short of the ready. Is that it? We all understand cash flow problems. But you still have to run this place, it shouldn't affect your orders to Northways. Goes without saying you have credit.'

Johnny dropped a generous deposit of crumbs on the floor and looked around possessively. It dawned on him that he and the restaurant proprietor were not alone: that the two men now propped against the bar were too big and wide to be the usual run of waiters, and it was not the time of day for gourmet customers.

'M'sieur Ettrick,' pleaded de Laubinque, 'I have no choice.'

Hanley pushed himself away from the bar. Denton brought up the rear.

Hanley said: 'Up.'

Johnny Ettrick did not know their faces, but he knew the type well enough – he and his brother had been surrounded by their own collection of them for long enough – and knew, too late, what he had walked into.

He got up.

Hanley and Denton accompanied him to the door. Out of nowhere appeared a third man, just to be on the safe side.

When the door opened, Johnny could hear the sobbing and wailing right across the street. The blonde girl was hunched up on the kerb, squealing hysterically. After one glance at the mess on the road beside her, Johnny could have done some hysterical squealing on his own account. The cherished, once spotless Porsche had somehow been turned upside down. Its windscreen had somehow got bashed inwards. The panels weren't what they had been such a short time ago, and the tyres thrusting up aimlessly to get a grip on the air were dangling a few ribbons here and there.

It was the end, the bloody end. Nothing in his life had ever hit him like this. Nothing could ever be worse. Or so he thought until Hanley and Denton elbowed him remorselessly into an alleyway.

Which left Colin Ettrick, as George Payne complacently commented to himself, to pick up the pieces: the pieces of his brother and the pieces of his brother's car. The Porsche could be attended to in Colin's garage, where a lot of criminal damage had been tidied up in the past and charged for accordingly. Tidying up Johnny was going to take a lot longer.

George Payne regretted not having his own personal fly

on the Ettrick garage wall to report back. But he could imagine most of it. You pull the right string, you have a pretty good idea how the puppet is going to kick. Colin Ettrick would have had no doubts about the meaning of this newest bit of message. He would be getting scared, or mad, or both. He would ask himself why it was the kid brother who had got mangled rather than himself; and he would know the answer, know that Payne was keeping him dangling, giving him one last chance of talking to whoever was now sorting out the local mafia problems. Santangelo had been obliterated. Johnny Ettrick had been beaten to within an inch of his life. The message was that Colin should waste no time in getting rid of Rafaello or whoever else was hoping to step into Santangelo's dangerous shoes.

Let Colin Ettrick get excited. Let him get so mad that he would come at the opposition like a mad bull. Wind him up so that he would make every mistake in the book. Two Ettricks and the Sicilians: a lot to handle, but Payne quite relished the idea of handling them. This was one of the factors that had brought him back on to his old territory: actually to be on the spot, *making* it all happen rather than giving remote instructions and waiting for reports that it *had* happened, like being dependent on television or radio news bulletins from distant parts.

George Payne could still show them a thing or two. He could enjoy every minute of it, even if it was getting a mite rougher than he had originally anticipated.

It was more fun than dealing with the small fry; but the small fry presented their own little characteristics, their own contributions to the whole *cataplana*.

Cavan nosed his Astra along the street, trying to ignore the irritable punching of a horn behind him. Somebody passed and glared across. He continued crawling along the kerb until at last he identified the entrance he had been told about. His hands were so sticky and shaky on the wheel that the Astra almost scraped the pillar at the top of the ramp. Then he was planing down to the dimly lit level with a few vacant parking spaces to either side.

Hanley stood there waiting for him. 'Don't get out of the motor.'

'Where's my wife?' Cavan croaked, winding down his window.

'Where's the photos?'

'My wife. You promised.'

A black coupé edged out of a slot at the far end of the car park. It came towards Cavan at a leisurely walking pace – which was appropriate enough, because Madeleine Cavan was handcuffed to the handle of the passenger door and could just keep pace with it, waving her free hand to keep her balance.

Cavan gagged, tried to get out of the Astra, found Hanley propped heavily against it with his right hand in through the open window.

'Photos.'

Cavan groped for his brief-case. His fingers slithered twice over the catch before he could get a grip and open it. There was something like pleasure, a crazy relief, when he handed over the pictures of the corridors and store-rooms. They were off his hands, no longer smouldering away like a time bomb in his case.

Hanley tilted one against the fitful light. 'This the central security area?'

'Part of it.'

'We want all of it.'

'But that's all I could possibly manage. It's enough to give you the general idea of –'

'All of it,' grated Hanley.

Cavan was sure he was going to be sick. He tried to gulp it back. After all he had done, they couldn't still be wanting more. Wanting the impossible. He was in the nightmare again, spluttering for words that would not come. Through the clogging suffocation he forced it out: 'You can't just stroll around in there without a reason. It takes proper authorization. What d'you think it's like – think I can walk in with a Polaroid flash, into one of the highest security buildings in Europe . . .?' Panic gripped his throat as he saw what the answer was going to be.

'Do exactly that,' said Hanley, 'unless you want we finish off your wife.'

Cavan tried to wrench out another protest, but the other car was already in reverse and Madeleine was tottering backwards, bouncing against the passenger door, twisting her right arm round to grab at the handle so that she would not be dragged along the concrete floor.

In a placating whine, yearning for it all somehow to be written off at one go, Cavan said: 'Listen. There's something else.'

'Yes?'

'I want to talk to your boss, whoever he is.'

'Who says I'm not the boss?'

'You're not.' It was the first and only time Cavan managed to feel a flicker of superiority over this burly thug. 'There has to be somebody behind you.'

'Everybody's a long way behind me,' said Hanley. But then he said: 'All right, you just say it to me and never mind anyone else. Just mind your own end of the business.'

'I gave you the schedule for a week from now. It's in there, all of it. Plus what I told you over the phone.'

'That's nothing new.'

'But something's happened. They're getting quicker off the mark with stuff they've seized. I thought they were cycling the schedule once every seven days. In fact it's been tightened up to once every five days.'

'So?'

'If you wanted to make the raid two days early, the security situation and movements are identical.'

Hanley stared at him as if to wring the last drop of truth out of him. 'Then all we need is the rest of the pictures, covering the whole area. And fast.'

All of which Hanely reported back to Monroe and George Payne, and waited for a pat on his bullet head. Payne simply nodded. His mind was beginning to tot up hours and minutes, facts and figures. So far he had found no reason to rely on computers: they lacked imagination and the willingness to readjust at a second's notice.

The phone rang. Monroe picked it up, grinned a sourly appreciative grin, and nodded at Payne to pick up the extension.

Colin Ettrick's voice erupted, almost spitting down the line. 'Are we going to talk about my brother?'

Monroe deferentially asked Payne a silent query. Payne magnanimously waved him to go ahead. Monroe said: 'Could be.'

'Then let me tell you something. You lot are in dead bother.' After a long pause without the whisper of a response, Ettrick burst out: 'What are you trying to do to me?'

'We're trying to make a point. About you and your Sicilians.'

'What sodding point?'

Payne smiled. It was all playing itself along, line by line, just as he had predicted. He mouthed a reply at Monroe, who said into the phone: 'If it's worrying you, let's discuss it. Let's meet with you and them.'

'Don't you lot understand about Sicilians? You take *one* out, you get *all of them* on top of you.' Ettrick was a raging bull now, all right, ready to go on the rampage. 'You've killed Santangelo, you think the rest of them are simply going to catch the first boat home?'

'As we understand it,' said Monroe suavely, 'Mr Rafaello is very much in charge now. I am sure he is capable of keeping things under control. We rather think he was always in charge. So we meet Rafaello and exchange views.'

'I don't believe this. How can you meet us – deal with us? You're in no position to pull any clever strokes, let me tell you that right now. My contacts with these people go back a long way.'

'We know all that, Colin. That's why you have the advantage.' Monroe paused as Payne pushed an architect's drawing towards him, turning it to emphasize one corner. 'Look, George has a new office building. Big empty place. No chance of being interrupted. Nothing naughty. Bring yourself, Mr Rafaello –'

'Oh, yes? And where is this dump?'

'Bridgetown House. *You* must have heard of it, Colin.' Monroe's voice was insinuating, his smile lethal. 'In the new South Bank development.'

'Yeah, I know it, of course I know it. But if you think the two of us are going to walk in there and –'

'Bring a hundred of your closest and most intimate friends, if that'll make you feel any more comfortable.'

'And you lot?'

'There'll just be the two of us. You must agree we've now reached the point where we've got to communicate sensibly with each other.'

Payne nodded approval. Sensible communication was what it was all about.

9 The sun struck across Middle Temple Lane on to the neatly cropped lawns and struck shimmering sparks from the fountain. Colonel Railton had chosen a bench which gave him a view down on to Garden Court, with a glimpse to one side of an arched doorway whose ecclesiastical style added to the sensation of being secluded in a medieval cloister in spite of the rumble of traffic along the Embankment. He was sitting there, his grey eyes appreciative yet troubled under his silvery hair, when John Miller came down the path and across the grass.

'Sorry, John. I couldn't ask counsel to wait any longer. He has a court appearance.'

Miller sat down beside him. 'I haven't got long. How did it go?'

His father-in-law hesitated, then said: 'It's all right. I'm sure it's going to be all right.'

'You really feel that?'

Railton was too staunchly honest a man to indulge in meaningless, reassuring noises. 'I don't know. It's like' – he fumbled, not used to expressing his emotions too openly –'an intermittent bad dream, really. You feel you're in charge one minute, and then there's the . . . uncertainty.'

'Fear,' said Miller quietly.

He looked around, seeing the same entrancing view and the same dignified buildings as Railton had been contemplating, but getting less pleasure from them. He knew too much of what went on behind those doors and windows before it got transferred across the road into the Law Courts. All too soon he was going to be involved in that squalid sort of thing himself. The mellowness of these buildings and the decorous manner of two men in gowns pacing towards a doorway into chambers were all very well for the casual observer: but here men dealt, day in, day out, with pain, suffering, despair and hatred, and made a handsome living out of it.

'We've got to go through with it,' said Railton with a childlike wonder at the misery of it all, 'because ... well, because we've got to.'

'I appreciate the way you're standing by me,' said Miller awkwardly. 'After all, she's your daughter, you might –' ·

'We're thinking about *your* daughter. My grand-daughter. You think I want her carted out of the country on some selfish whim, not see her for God knows how long?'

A cloud drifted across the sun and cast a slowly dragging shadow over the bench.

Miller said: 'Did he give you any idea what sort of contact he'd had with Vanessa's lawyer?'

'None whatsoever. He was a little surprised about that.'

So, thought Miller, they still had nothing but Vanessa telling him on the phone, breathlessly and in a guilty rush, pretending she couldn't talk long because it was an expensive call, that she was sorry but she'd done a lot of thinking and she was going to leave England for good and take Abigail to Ireland with her. Abigail wouldn't suffer: Seamus was truly very, very fond of her. Like that earlier communication, the scrawled letter telling him about Seamus and hoping he would understand and forgive her and not make difficulties over the divorce. Like Vanessa every time, through and through – doing whatever came into her head, ignoring everybody else and every other interest, not bothering to attempt even the most basic rational explanation. Certainly never bothering to behave like a civilized, responsible human being.

It was difficult to hold on to her, or shake sense into her, or strike back when you could not even get a grip on her.

'Nothing definite about Ireland?' he ventured.

'Nothing. Not a word from her lawyer. I'd like to think,' Railton went on wistfully, 'that it all means she's changed her mind, that the whole wretched business is all over and she's ashamed of herself. Which she damn well ought to be.' The sunlight flowed across the grass towards them once more. 'If she did, would you perhaps consider . . . well . . .'

Railton's voice trailed away. Miller could not fill in the silence. He didn't know what the answer would be. It wasn't something he could even begin to think about until the proposition was put to him by Vanessa herself. And there was no indication that it was likely to be.

It was a bit late now to start retracing one's steps.

Railton sighed. 'Well, there doesn't seem much point in hanging about. I'll head for home.'

'You're definitely going back to the country now?'

'I can do with getting this stale city air out of my lungs. Don't know how you stand it. I'll go and breathe some fresh air, build up my strength for our court appearance.' He was trying to make a gallant joke out of it. Abruptly he added: 'Counsel says you're not to speak to Vanessa before the hearing.'

'Wouldn't dream of it.' So much for any faint possibility of it all somehow sorting itself out. 'But,' said Miller stonily, 'I'll certainly speak to her after. At some length.'

Colonel Railton got up. 'Depending on how long she'll listen. Not much of a gel for staying put and listening, wouldn't you agree?'

They gazed glumly down the steps and the path to the gate on the Embankment.

'I'll drive you to the station,' Miller offered. 'It's not all that far out of my way.'

'You'll do no such thing. In a police vehicle? More than my reputation's worth – and maybe your job?' Railton clumsily squeezed his son-in-law's arm. 'I'm going to take a stroll round these beautiful gardens and then go gently on my way.'

'You're sure?'

'Sure. Phone me later.'

'I will. If anything crops up. . . .' Miller left it hanging on the air, then moved away and set off back to the London Embassy Hotel.

He half expected to see Collis cruising around in the Sierra, but there was no sign of him. It took Miller a few minutes to notice Detective Sergeant Meg Richards in a Maestro parked well back from the hotel. She wound her window down as he approached. Inside there was the faint murmur of the portable UHF receiver, recording a meeting going on in the room upstairs.

Richards nodded into the middle distance but said nothing, letting Miller take the conversation in.

'We really do have to have an end-use prospect on site for the twenty-four thousand feet on rear mezzanine, block three.'

'That means going through a whole "change of use".'

'I know that.'

'You say rear mezzanine, but twenty-four thousand is a third of the area of block three. I mean, bugger it, this is delay. Let's build for approved spec, *then* put in for change of use.'

'It's a decision we don't have to take now. What I think we have to discuss is this Saudi money, refinancing site option loan.'

'I think Charlie got us done for a good sixteen and a half per cent.'

'Well, it looked cheap at the time. What d'you think, Mr Payne?'

Meg Richards mouthed the word 'Payne' at Miller with a questioning lift of her eyebrows.

It was a name that meant nothing in itself. It could have been any of that little clique in there. But Miller got the sniff of it. Hanrahan? Payne? Whatever the tie-up was, there was always the chance of two fellers being one feller. But all this financial stuff sounded a long way from the drugs dealings they were after. Maybe somebody back on the fourth floor could analyse it.

114

The R/T in his own vehicle crackled into life. He nipped back to his seat, in time to be summond back to the Yard.

On his way through, a phone jangled and DI Mackie was waving at him. 'Old friend of yours.'

Miller did not understand the wry smirk as he took the receiver.

'John.' It was Collis's voice.

'Where are you?'

'Westminster Hospital.'

Miller was about to comment that he thought Collis had been told to keep away from the hospital, but realized in time that Mackie, carefully engrossed in paperwork, was equally carefully listening.

'How's things, then?'

'Still the same.'

'And what about the target? What about Monroe's chum? A fair chance he's back in the hotel without you.'

'That's something I want to talk to you about. I want to have a word with the doc here, then I'll grab a cab.'

'Cab? Where's the motor?'

Mackie made an odd little snorting noise, and seemed to find something wildly amusing on the sheet of paper before him.

Collis said: 'It's down an embankment.'

'Embankment?' Miller thought he had misheard. 'The tube station? But I was there myself not a –'

'The car,' said Collis, 'is down a big embankment.'

'You mean you've had an accident?'

Mackie sat back and abandoned all pretence of being engrossed elsehwere.

'It's off the road. Down a slope. Or it was. They ought to have dragged it back up. This time maybe they've been lucky.'

Miller let out an incredulous breath. 'What state are you in?'

'Oh, terrific, of course.'

'And the car?'

'Not a pretty sight.'

'All right. How did it happen?'

'Shit. I was following those two guys – Monroe and whoever. Crammed on the speed. I ... well, I overtook someone on the inside, and ... oh, what the hell, never mind the inquest. It's a mess, that's enough.'

'You'd better get back in here,' said Miller, 'as soon as you can.'

As he replaced the receiver he saw the derisive gleam in Mackie's eye. 'A bit of a naughty boy, our Jim,' he said with relish. 'That's a whole fleet of motors he's totalled in the last twelve months.'

'Only two,' Miller corrected him.

'*Only* two.' Mackie savoured the irony of this, then said: 'Right, now you're back ... you got that name back there – Payne?'

'I was going to ask about that.'

'We've already asked. And got it. Things are shaping up very attractively. Your toothpaste tube, for a start. Quite an acquisition, that. Get along to the darkroom and the video lab. Shaw and Wright. The two of them will spell it out for you. Even without Wright's electronics, you may suss out what two plus two can be made to add up to.'

Miller went along to the darkroom, where DS Shaw was waiting with that impatience which only the most pampered technicians and specialists enjoy displaying, in any walk of life. Shaw, flicking his tongue derisively against his teeth, gave Miller about five seconds to sit down and get his breath back before flicking on the infra-red.

'These picture of yours outside the hotel. This one here ... this Astra ... just what are you asking for?'

Miller gloomily contemplated the car side-on, its front number-plate at such a slant that none of the letters or figures could be made out.

'Hell. Any chance of getting a decent angle on that number-plate?'

Shaw sniffed. 'I tell you who might cope with this, if they've got nothing else on their plate. And that's NASA in dear old downtown Houston. We've had some very fine photo and image enhancement from them at one time and another. But it takes time. And no doubt we're all in a mad hurry, as usual?'

'As usual,' Miller confirmed.

'I'll flat the plate with an anamorphic. Then I'll put it on video and we'll have a shot at image-enhancing.'

'How long?'

'Miracles don't come in ten minutes. But at least I should manage a pretty good blow-up of your photos.' As he virtually dismissed Miller from his august presence, he remembered: 'Oh, Wright next door's got something to show you. Might cheer you up a bit.'

Wright, a tried and true electronics whiz-kid, was less lofty than Shaw, a lot more committed to idolatry of the equipment he played on like Oscar Peterson in particular exhilarated mood.

He had come up with a beaut. Miller leaned admiringly over it. 'Mackie said you'd got a result. Do we get to know who and what?'

It was a magnified fingerprint from the tube he had extracted from that bathroom in the London Embassy Hotel. It merited more than the muted praise Mackie had bestowed on it a few minutes ago. If there was a similar one on record, it ought to have been child's play to match them.

'I'm told that the name is George Edward Payne,' said Wright.

Collis slipped into the room behind them. Together they studied the print with all the awe which a connoisseur might feel when confronted with a hiterto unidentified but genuine Giotto.

'Payne?' Collis echoed.

'Almost no form at all,' Wright recited. 'But a lot of whispers. A GBH way back. Tucked up for fourteen months. Apart from that, clean, according to your lot. And rich.'

'It shows.'

'Name features on any number of building and development companies,' contributed Mackie from the doorway. 'But we haven't established what they all tie in with, if anything.'

Miller said: 'He has a yacht?'

'He does indeed. Lloyd's registered. One reference to it being a few miles along the coast from Faro, and a sighting off Marbella. Not confirmed, though.'

'It figures,' said Collis reverently.

Mackie waved a positively avuncular hand and left them to it.

In spite of his disclaimer about miracles, Shaw reappeared in less time than Miller had dared to hope. He displayed a twenty-two-inch visual of the front of the London Embassy, sharply defined and with star cast – the lawyer, the man they had established as David Monroe, and alongside the odd little man and his Astra with the coyly evasive number-plate. Collis shrugged a question at Miller, who shrugged back. It was Wright who, careful not to tread on Shaw's sensitive toes, suggested they put the photo on video and feed it through the computer. Between them, though, they could promise no enchantment that would swivel the car obligingly round to present them with a lovely head-on view.

'All the same,' said Shaw peevishly, 'I'd have thought there was enough there to provide you with *some* details to work on.'

It was the tinge of sarcasm which prompted Miller to take him up on it. 'One thing you could try. Pull right out. Try and enhance the right of the windscreen. Area of licence disc.'

Shaw glowered for a moment, but Wright applied himself with the enthusiasm of the true craftsman. He wound the focus back to the original picture of the man heading towards his Astra, then pulled out and on to the area around the disc within the car's windscreen. From the blur there emerged a pale yet clearer image.

'Look!' breathed Miller.

Tucked in behind the licence was a parking permit. The picture enlarged, and there it was, fuzzy but unmistakeable: *Customs and Excise, Heathrow.*

Again Miller and Collis exchanged glances. Just what the hell did this mean?

Across the road from the London Embassy Hotel a block of shops and offices reared above the slip road which Miller and Collis had used for surveillance once or twice in the Sierra which was now of little immediate use. In the London Embassy there was a bank of swift, silent lifts. No lift served the block facing it: the whole row had been assembled piecemeal, with a number of flats tacked on above the terrace of shops and first-floor offices. One hallway and staircase served the office end, another the flats. At the back was an emergency concrete stairwell which went right to the top. Miller and Collis toiled up it by the light of bulkhead lamps in the walls, protected by thick bars. They were laden with camera and telephoto, a dish aerial, UHF receiver, and two folding chairs – 'So you can make yourselves comfortable,' as Mackie had observed, 'but not so comfortable you drowse off.'

They finally reached the attic. Miller unlocked a door.

Propping himself against the wall for a moment, Collis said: 'How come you've picked on that room; It faces the rear.'

'It faces the front.'

'I just looked out the window on that last landing, as we were coming up. This is to the back. View on the motorway.'

Miller opened the door and went in. Collis lumbered after him, waiting to triumph. The windows were dirty, but the lights along the front of the hotel blazed brightly through.

'If that's an example of your sense of direction,' said Miller, 'it's no wonder you ended up down an embankment.'

'That subject is taboo. Right off the menu.'

They began to set up the surveillancing equipment. Collis tuned the receiver, searching for Payne's bugged suite, and found it.

Somebody was saying: 'I wouldn't mind another drink.'

'Me neither,' murmured Collis.

'What would you like – a small Scotch?'

'Make mine a large one,' said Collis. 'What about you, John?'

'You're not drinking and driving.'

Collis made a face at the UHF speaker. 'Yes, I suppose I'd better make it a tomato juice.'

'A tomato juice,' said Miller, 'and a large guide dog for the blind.'

'I warned you. . . .'

They unfolded the chairs and set them up close to the window. Behind the voluminous net curtains of the bugged room they could see a flicker of acid blue light, and a shadow moving to and fro. Then somebody sat down, or disappeared into another corner of the room, while the television continued to slide smears of pallid light across the walls and curtain. The clink of glasses through the receiver produced a barely audible moan from Collis. Then a familar tune welled out.

'"Panorama",' he said.

'That's not "Panorama".'

'It is.'

'You've never watched "Panorama". It's right over your head.'

'I could have brought my little portable along.'

'This is a surveillance. You're not setting up house.'

'We might as well be comfortable.' Collis wriggled in his chair. 'Even Mackie agreed on that.'

'You want comfort? You half kill some poor bloke. You

park a police mobile down an embankment, by the grace of God not slaughtering any civilians, the bosses are screaming for your guts ... and you want to be comfortable.'

'Stop making lists. Especially of things I want to forget.' Collis opened one of the plastic bags and dug into it for a couple of small bottles of Malvern water and a packet of *grissini*.

Miller switched his attention from the room across the way. 'How many packets of breadsticks you got there?'

'None of your business.'

'Must be twenty, hm?'

'Nowhere near.'

'How can you kid yourself? You've been saying each packet is 160 calories –'

'It is.'

'Who says so?'

'I read it in a book. Or a magazine.' Collis tore a crackling slice of wrapper away and fished out a long stick, biting the end off it with an even louder crackling noise.

'It's not on the side of the packet, then?' When Collis did not reply, Miller went on remorselessly: 'There's breadsticks and breadsticks. I'm sure those little tiny ones, three to a packet, you get in Italian restaurants – all right, maybe *they're* 160. But those things you've got there are big, fat, thick ones. Say 600 calories.'

'Leave it off.'

'How many packs a day are you on now?'

Collis took another stick and crunched into it. 'Four,' he muttered.

'Six.'

'Aw, occasionally five.'

'Five times 600 calories is –'

'Times 160 calories,' Collis sharply corrected him.

'Which makes 3000. That's the equivalent of drinking a pint of grease. What was all that about your strict diet, and losing weight, and –'

'I've lost eight pounds in the two months since I started on breadsticks and salad.'

'Maybe you washed your socks.'

'A real comedian.'

Miller shook his head. 'No, we've got to face it. You're a genuine original. A bloke shoving breadsticks into his face twenty-four hours a day, visibly expanding by the minute . . . have you ever thought of psychiatric help?'

'Very humorous.' Collis was really needled by now. 'Let's shut up, shall we?'

'Answer me a question. When you were bawled out by the Commander yesterday, why did you go straight to that hot dog stand in Victoria Street?'

'You don't know I –'

'I know all right. And I think you should start to get worried when food is no longer something to burn to produce energy. To you food is solace, right? It's comfort. It's little naked baby Jimmy cradled in his mummy's arms.'

'Give it a rest.'

'And what about the shape of these breadsticks? Wouldn't you say the shape had certain psychological connotations?'

'That is enough,' said Collis, deadly.

'It is.' Miller craned forward. 'He's heading out.'

Someone had moved across the light of the television screen. The shape looked decidedly like that of George Edward Payne. Miller and Collis began to get up. But Payne stopped by the door and turned back towards the television.

'I'm serving notice,' grumbled Collis. 'If they watch it through to the Epilogue, and the lights go out, I'm off.'

'They're not in that hotel just to watch television.'

But the background drone of a commentator's voice went on, interrupted only by another clink of glasses. Collis slumped down as far as he was able in the restrictions of his chair. Whatever he was thinking about, it was nothing very cheering. While Miller found himself harking back to that unsatisfactory discussion with his father-in-law. The sensation was going to plague him for days, weeks, maybe forever: the perversity of fighting over a loved one with someone you'd once loved.

Trying to shake himself out of it, he said: 'How about you and the women? Haven't heard much from you since poor Jenny.'

It shook Collis out of himself as well. Clearly he had not given much thought to this topic recently. Now he stared reflectively back into the past, and found it not so displeasing in one or two aspects. 'I really miss Jenny,' he said, sounding a bit smug rather than despondent. 'I wouldn't mind having her round the place again. Ever since she left, the flat looks like a council tip.'

Here at any rate Miller could feel envy for Jim Collis. He had seen Collis's women come and go, liked some of them and been relieved when others vanished from the scene. It somehow seemed easy for Collis: pick up the new one, swear this was the real thing at last, enjoy a few months of passion laced with domesticity, and then get it all out of your system in a couple of flaming rows. None of the women had ever really looked permanent. There was an enviable security in that kind of impermanence. Miller recalled taking Vanessa round to the flat once, half expecting her to be shocked by the quarrel and parting that was obviously blowing up, and Collis's shamelessly outspoken praise of somebody else he had met. Instead she had been amused, getting on splendidly with Collis and the soon-to-be-discarded girl, almost in complicity with them. Miller had not even guessed at the time just how ready Vanessa herself was to ditch everything and go off.

He said: 'All it really means to you is having someone around to keep the bed warm and the place tidy?'

'You can get over-subtle with women.'

'Not you. *I* can. Not you.'

'Did it never occur to you that if you'd once thrown your old lady out of the front door at dawn, in the middle of a storm, in her nightdress, you might have sorted out many of the deeper intellectual arguments?'

'No, it didn't occur.'

'I know I may sound old-fashioned –'

'No,' said Miller forcefully, 'you don't sound old-fashioned: you just sound like an idiot.'

'If you look at the scoreboard, I think you'll find I've done better than you.'

Not a scoreboard, thought Miller bleakly: it had nothing to do with scoring. He ought to be somewhere else, devoting his time to reasoning the whole thing through, somehow taking charge and restoring everything to what it ought to be, instead of squatting here watching a hotel frontage and one particular window, listening to meaningless noises. All this to make a living . . . for someone who was no longer interested in the living or in his own life.

All at once the television glow faded, and the room lights went out.

Collis and Miller were on their feet, thudding down the stairs. They reached the car – an Escort to replace the crippled Sierra – as Payne and Monroe came out through the front doors of the hotel and down the steps to a waiting grey Mercedes. Miller was ready, his foot poised for the off, as the two men got into their car. But then, having settled themselves, they just sat there – waiting for some signal, some message to start them on their way?

'We should've bugged the car.'

'Too late,' shrugged Collis.

'Did you check out a gun?'

'No. *You* got one?'

'I kept it from yesterday. Why didn't you ask Mackie if you could check one out?'

'You're the blue-eyed boy right now, not me. I daren't ask Mackie for anything. Haldane won't even give me the time of day since I put the motor down the Matterhorn. I'm a leper.'

'You've got one chance.'

Collis stared greedily at the motionless Merc. 'I know what you're going to say.'

'If we pull off George Payne and the connection to the stuff into Heathrow,' said Miller slowly and deliberately, 'then you're in on a spectacular result. And they can't fire you.'

'Let's see it happen, that's all I ask.'

'We'll do it,' said Miller. 'We'll do it together.'

Whatever signal Payne and Monroe had been waiting for, it must have come. The Mercedes was rolling forward. Then it stopped, as if someone had had second thoughts. Payne got out and went towards the doorman, who saluted briefly and came down two steps, looking along the street for a taxi.

The Mercedes set off again.

'On Payne,' asked Collis, 'or the other?'

Either decision could be the wrong one. No decision at all would be fatal. Miller set off in pursuit of the Merc.

They followed it through Fulham to a corner pub, where it stopped with the engine still running. Three heavies came out of the pub, spoke for a few seconds with Monroe, nodded obediently, and headed for a Ford van parked ten yards down a side street. The Mercedes resumed its journey with the van close behind and the Escort discreetly further back.

The next stop was outside a mews garage in Pimlico. Three men who had apparently been working unusually late hours tramped across the inspection bay, pulled the doors shut, and piled into the van. The procession set off again.

'This is one hell of a rally,' said Collis. 'What's all that muscle power for?'

Miller reached for the handset as he drove. 'MP, MP from central four-four.'

'Go ahead, central four-four.'

'Is Inspector Mackie available? Urgent. Can I speak direct?'

'Give us a minute.' It was an endless minute, then: 'Central four-four. Go ahead.'

'Sir, it's Miller.'

'Yes, John?'

Collis grimaced at the familiarity.

'We've got a potential problem,' Miller said. 'We've followed target. They've toured Fulham into Pimlico, picking up faces along the way. With the drivers, eight at least. We're driving down Gunter Grove, in a line. If they split and we want to follow all, we need at least six-up support.'

'You know the answer to that. Chances of me finding three spare mobiles for Chelsea area are poor. I'll see what I can do. Report immediately they reach destination.'

'Right, guv. Out.'

Collis said: 'And if they do split up, which way do we dive?'

'Have to play it by ear.'

In Vauxhall Bridge Road a Rover 3500 parked outside a pub eased itself into the convoy. Still they were all together.

'Gathering of the hooligan clans,' observed Miller.

'Answer me a question.' Collis was studying the vehicles ahead with mounting concern. Pretty heavy odds against two coppers, one of them unarmed. 'This George Edward Payne character. Big property dealer – that's what we were told, isn't it? Why's a man like that connected with a bunch of wallies caught with heroin into Heathrow?'

Miller had no answer to that one. Not yet. Whatever the operation was, it had to be pretty big to lure in a man like Payne. And come to think of it, where the hell was Payne himself by this time?

10 George Payne reached the sixth floor of Bridge-town House and stepped on to the vast concrete space of what would one day be divided up into executive offices with views along the South Bank and across the Thames. The floor would be served by high-speed lifts, superior to the two available at the moment: an external builder's cage crawling up the wall of the building, shielded only by an expanse of polythene sheeting which flapped and moaned to itself in the evening breeze, and an internal service lift which was not supposed to be in working order yet – though Payne knew better.

Through a corner joint of the plastic he could see car lights twinkling and fussing to and fro along the Em-bankment and over the bridges. A train dragged a streamer of brightness along a railway viaduct. And, blurred by the polythene curtain, there was a turmoil of light along the rim of the derelict site below and around the foundations of new buildings. In daylight or at night it was a good place to be, if only he could have spared the time to watch every stage in the project's growth and to see beyond it to other sites he would soon own, the houses he would pull down, and to see in his mind's eye what would rise from their ruins.

Headlights of a car swerved in directly below him, little glow-worms jigging and then settling on to the hardpacked earth beside a mound of rubble. Brake lights winked red and then were extinguished.

Hanley was down there, waiting to receive their visitors. He carried two walkie-talkies, through one of them re-porting each movement to Payne in his eyrie. As the car with the two Italians in it drew up and stopped he had emerged from the shadows of the basement ramp but did not come out too far. From here there was a view under

127

the railway arches: enough of a view to show a Volvo coming towards them, and two more motors behind. Colin Ettrick and two of his hoods got out of the Volvo. The other vehicles began disgorging another half-dozen of his heavy mob. Hanley did his sums and murmured the numbers into the transmitter. The men picked their way heavily past the builders' hut to form a semi-circle confronting Hanley. Rafaello and Lombardi got out of their De Tomaso Deauville to join them.

Hanley kept them waiting half a minute, then said: 'This is an empty building.'

'It had better be,' said Ettrick.

'Check it. Mr Payne and Mr Monroe are up on the top floor. Lovely view of the river. Why don't you send one of yours up? They can give you the report that it's all kosher.'

He held out the walkie-talkies. Ettrick studied them dubiously, then signed to two of his heavies. One of them took a walkie-talkie, and they went into the lift and pressed the button. As it went grinding its way up, a flurry of rain slapped and rattled across the polythene cocoon.

Feet shuffled on the earth as they waited. Ettrick kept his eyes on Hanley, and his ear close to the walkie-talkie. One false move and there would be no more talking.

Ettrick said something terse into the radio, listened, grunted and spoke again.

A car slowed near the entrance through the fence. Hanley identified the outline of an Escort – another of Ettrick's back-up team? – but it accelerated and turned a corner, and any further sound it might have made was drowned by the wind and the squeal of the lift descending again.

Ettrick's men tensed.

The hoods came out of the cage, and made way for Ettrick and the two Italians to go up.

Rain spattered again. The lift ascended.

At the top, Payne and Monroe stood in the half light like diplomats in a huge reception hall waiting to shake hands with their guests. Ettrick, a few paces ahead of Rafaello and Lombardi, made no move to shake hands. The two groups stayed well apart, a no-man's-land of cold cement between them.

Payne broke the silence. 'This building is one item in a hundred-million-pound development. I'm the major partner in the consortium. I'm a substantial man, *Mister* Ettrick.'

None of the three replied, but Rafaello looked covertly around at the shell of the vast block. A gust of wind boomed against the polythene, and dust was blown along the floor.

'Now,' Payne went on, 'about our meeting at the cinema. I got the impression you weren't taking me seriously.' He addressed himself directly, harshly, at Ettrick. 'Some employee of mine may have misinterpreted some later observations of mine and felt it his duty to attack your brother. Unfortunate.'

Rafaello's gaze was solely on Payne now. 'You killed Mr Santangelo. Was that also *unfortunate*?'

'Or did I supply your wish fulfilment for you?' asked Payne, suddenly gentle and insinuating. 'Santangelo was "old family" style. He would never listen to the kind of deal we've got to discuss.'

'Which is . . .?'

'You buy your heroin from here, your coca from there. Sometimes the price is low, sometimes high. I can give you all the heroin you'll need for three years for the UK, at a fixed low price.'

Rafaello shifted his weight from one foot to the other. He edged up to take his place on a level with Ettrick. 'But do we want to deal with you?'

'If you don't, someone else will.'

'Nobody deals with you' – Rafaello was matching Payne's gentleness – 'if you're removed from the scene.'

'It's 1986. Let's be intelligent. We have all the elements to make a deal.'

'I don't think you understand,' Ettrick exploded. 'You're getting this the wrong way round. It's me and him who'll offer *you* a deal. Not you offer us.'

'You keep your silence a minute,' said Rafaello. 'Let this man talk.'

'You going to let him con you? This bastard tried to murder my brother. And he *did* murder your Signor Santangelo.'

Rafaello glanced at Lombardi for confirmation, then said: 'Ettrick, calm down.'

Ettrick was in no mood to calm down. 'You'd do a deal *he* offers? That's not my idea, son.'

'Then,' said Payne to Rafaello, across Ettrick, 'we may have to think of your friend here as optional.'

'Sod you. Don't you talk about me like that.'

'Go away.'

Ettrick glared at Rafaello, demanding his support. After a brief hesitation Rafaello said: 'Leave us.'

'Bloody right I'll leave you. Right in the shit where you'll get yourself.'

'I will talk to our Mr Payne. Then you.'

Ettrick stormed towards the end of the floor and got into the lift, jabbing furiously at the button. As he disappeared from view, Payne said: 'I repeat the point. I have the merchandise. It's destined for the streets.'

'Is it?' Rafaello challenged. 'Have you got that much heroin now? In your possession?' When there was no reply he went on more forcefully: 'Suppose I say I want it now, I want to buy all of it? How much you got, right now? What's your answer?'

'Not yet. A little while.' Payne smiled to himself. It was such a beautiful concept, it produced such a warming sensation at the back of the mind and right down to the stomach.

'Which mean someone else has got it, yes? Our contacts in this area are excellent. If someone has this amazing quantity of heroin for sale, is no trouble: we can identify the source.'

'I don't think it's a source you'll identify.'

Rafaello appeared to be turning this over. But there was something in his face that, even in these shadows, Payne could recognize. Maybe the shadows on those dark features merely served to make it clearer, accentuate it. Rafaello was simply weighing up the business deal against the question of whether George Payne should be allowed to survive.

He took his time. At last, without even consulting Lombardi, he said: 'I'm going to have to think about it. I consult with my associates, you understand? And then we talk again.'

Payne knew he had been right. What Rafaello was really saying was 'No'. He glanced at Monroe, who licked his lips, took a deep breath, and moved forward a pace.

Shadows moved out of the service lift at the far end of the floor.

There was an awful lot of automobile horse-power in there, and a hefty complement of manpower, but not much activity to show for it. Miller and Collis were uneasy. There was no way the two of them could risk marching straight in and helping themselves to a trip in the lift which they had seen go up and down. But sitting here would show them nothing.

Miller opened his door. Without a word Collis got out. They hugged the fence as they approached the site entrance. A builders' hut shielded the men beyond, and hid the two sergeants from those men.

Even from this vantage point there was little to be seen over the landscape of rubble, excavators, and other hunched machinery. Only another descent of the lift, and a glimpse of Colin Ettrick getting out. There was some sort of discussion around the foot of the lift shaft, and Ettrick was waving his heavies into a new formation, closer to the lift, waiting. . . .

Miller bent over his personal W/T. 'DS Miller. Repeat

previous message. Urgent – repeat urgent – need of re-inforcements at same location.'

'MP to DS Miller. Message received. Mobiles, two, on way to you. Urgentest. Hold on. Message ends.'

Hold on! Easy to say, all that way away, thought Miller sourly. He eased the gun out into his hand, half extending it to Collis. Collis shook his head. Miller waved to him to skirt right round the site clockwise, while he moved in from the right in a shorter approach under cover of the building.

Still not much to see. No arguments, no punch-ups. Just those lumps of muscle standing about, not sure of what they were supposed to be doing or what was likely to happen next. Ettrick looked round again, missing some-body or something. The two Italians were not yet down, and Payne's man, Hanley, had gone.

Skittish rain swirled across from the river; the polythene creaked and billowed and boomed again. Miller tried to make out who was missing from the windswept scene, and why.

Somewhere far along the side of the building he thought he saw two grey figures emerge from an exit which might have served a lift. So was there another lift inside, in working order?

At the same time the builders' lift came down again and squeaked to a stop.

Ettrick turned to look, waiting for the two Mafiosi to get out.

The gate opened.

Miller saw Ettrick and one of his men stare into the cage. Then Ettrick had his hand to his mouth, and was lurching away to one side. Behind him, one of his hoods let out a howl which was caught up by the wind and tossed mockingly against the translucent sheeting.

All at once they were all running, panicking, as if they had seen a bomb waiting to go off in their faces.

Miller saw, through the scaffolding, a car start up and

leave fast, very fast. It was the Mercedes which had brought Payne and Monroe here. Ettrick's mob were scrambling off in the opposite direction, oblivious to the Merc's departure.

Miller's right hand pushed against the wall of the building to give him extra impetus as he sprinted round the corner towards the lift, to see what they had seen. Collis was closing in from the far side, crouching low but racing like an agile retriever over the hummocks of rubble, joining him near the open gate of the lift cage.

Inside was the explanation of Ettrick's panic. Propped upright against one side of the cage was Rafaello, a bullet hole between the eyes and a spreading shadow behind him which might have been the contents of his head. Sprawled across the floor was his sidekick, face down in a pool of blood.

11 Colonel Railton had been afraid of an explosion when his daughter and son-in-law at last confronted each other across the table at the hearing, face to face for the first time since Vanessa had made her threat to take Abigail away. John Miller himself had been none too sure of how he might react. He had gone into the room this morning in that state of mingled apprehension and tight-chested savagery which had carried him through many a murderous situation, only this time it was all going to be more personal, the real hand-to-hand combat.

Yet now they were here, he felt drained: nothing more.

There she was, pale and distrait on the other side of the table. You couldn't start yelling insults at her. The whole atmosphere was informal but serious: not a fight but a civilized discussion. The judge sat without a wig at the head of the table, smiling benignly. The two lawyers nodded to each other in the friendliest fashion. Violent scenes were not in keeping with these well-meaning procedures.

Vanessa's counsel was saying: 'And in view of the fact that my client now wishes to re-marry and make a new home in the Republic of Ireland, it is obviously in the child's best interests to be with her mother in a stable family environment.'

Stable family environment . . . with a feckless Irishman, a distiller's marketing manager who would probably be away from home as much as Miller had been and maybe for longer periods? That was how the bloody conniving Mick had met Vanessa and seized his opportunity, and seized her body, and touched, and coaxed out of her all that Miller had known and . . .

The bastard. There would be plenty more opportunities for a lousy lecherous leprechaun like that. With his mobility and his expense account, he could score whenever it took his fancy. And Vanessa would learn: learn to be bored again, resentful again – and who would *her* next one be?

His gaze tried to challenge hers across the table. But her eyes were lowered, unhappy and evasive. Sly bitch. Until the very last minute she had played it clever, said as little as possible, answered no communications. Now her nerve was almost failing her. Miller sensed it, knew her: he had known everything there was to know about her. Her high cheekbones, which had so often given her a captivating arrogance, now looked painfully close to the surface of pallid, tightly drawn skin. Served her bloody well right. Let her find out what unhappiness meant. Let her find out how long it could last, with you every hour of the day and deep into the night.

She didn't have to be unhappy. If he just got up and walked round the table and put his arms round her and told her to stop being so bloody-minded and told the rest of them to piss off, surely it would make sense to everybody in the end. Most of all to themselves.

But it was too late to make any of that ring true. And there was no way now of interrupting that smug penguin, droning on: 'My client wishes to make it clear that she is prepared to allow the father reasonable access to the child at intervals arranged at their mutual convenience. She would also consider allowing the child to visit the father for suitable holiday periods if Mr Miller's other duties did not preclude his giving the child his full attention at such times.'

Suitable holiday periods . . . meaning times when she and her pet Mick wanted to get away together without being bothered by a little girl . . . or she wanted to accompany him on his business trips and keep a good grip on him.

Miller opened his mouth, on the verge of a snarl, but heard a warning cough from Railton close to his shoulder.

'Questions of maintenance for the child were, of course, amicably settled during the earlier divorce proceedings.'

Of course. So amicably.

Look, you silly spoilt bitch, so I didn't give Abigail my full attention – that's the insinuation, creeping in for the hundredth time, isn't it? – *couldn't* give her my full loving attention while I was sweating my guts out to make a comfortable life for her and the two of us. It's what you wanted at the start – what you drooled over – the tough go-getting copper who swept you off your feet, came home with stories of blood and violence, fought his way to early promotion and more money so we could get a decent house to live in and bring up Abigail and any others who came along later. Only when you saw that the right income meant hard work and long hours, that was different. That was something to be sneered at, snapped at. Go on, look at me. Do you think it'll be any different for you next time round? Do you really think that your randy wheeler-dealer from Wicklow . . .

'There has never been more than a flimsy suggestion that the ex Mrs Miller was anything but an admirable mother. During her occasional absences she ensured, with the support of her father, that a nanny was provided to give adequate care. For the rest of the time, her own personal devotion has never been in question.'

But she wasn't going to get Abigail. Christ, there had to be some justice in the world: wasn't that what his own job was supposed to be all about? Miller listened to the bland blathering without truly hearing any of it; and clung to the belief that the truth was the truth and must surely prevail.

The judge was raising a question which meant nothing to Miller. It must have been some esoteric technicality. Certainly it interested the judge and the two lawyers more than the actual people in the case appeared to have done. They smiled polite excuses to Miller, Railton and Vanessa, and put their heads together.

Miller found himself wondering what was waiting for him back on the fourth floor. That had been a pretty bloody conclusion to last night's efforts. The way things were going, this would turn out to be one of those investigations in which they'd be choked by sheer input. Four murders in a little over forty-eight hours, and still no sign of an identifiable wood through the trees. What were they missing? Maybe Cannock and Haldane and the rest of the top brains would have found the answers by the time he reported back for duty. Add three dead Italians and a hitman, to a Turk, a Cypriot, an Algerian and a handful of Pakistanis carting bags of skag through Heathrow, and what did you get? All along it had had the makings of a first division game. Now it looked like being a cup tie. A pity it was so hard to tell who was playing whom – and God alone knew who the ref might be, and how much he could be relied on.

When he got back to the Yard. . . .

Miller jerked his attention back to the proceedings in this decorous room, where everybody else except himself and Vanessa were so friendly and there were so many courteous, encouraging smiles being tossed about. My learned friend this, my learned friend that. . . .

At last Taylor was on his feet. About time he began earning his fee. But still he preserved that civil, relaxed air, summing up with more obvious pleasure in his own expertise than in the justice of his client's case.

'In conclusion, Your Honour, I believe Mr Miller's claim is based on impermeable argument. Here is a man, a detective sergeant of outstanding record in the police force of this metropolis, a man of the highest moral standards, a person of such integrity that he is supported in this action by his ex-wife's own father, Colonel Michael Railton. I am sure we will all have noted and been gratified by the absence of hysterical scenes on either side. There have been no unblanced recriminations, nothing but the sad reportage of facts – too long a string of undeniable facts, all of them tending inevitably towards one interpretation and one only. The truth has surely shone through. You have heard Mr Railton describe the behaviour of his daughter – his own daughter – a mother who went off for a week's ski-ing holiday, with the generous approval of her overworked husband. A week which turned into a month's holiday with some lover. Only one phone call home during that month to enquire about the health and welfare of her baby daughter.'

Vanessa's head rose. She stared full at John Miller, bitterly, as though her indifference had somehow been all his fault: it was he and not she who had been guilty of indifference.

'And after the divorce, when with Mr Miller's tolerant consent she yet again had free access to her child, she went yet again for protracted holidays in the Alps and elsewhere, during which time she was quite content to unload her responsibilities on to her ex-husband and her father. We cannot seriously consider,' Taylor pleaded, 'that Your Honour would look favourably upon any application to allow Mr Miller's child to be taken out of her own country to the Republic of Ireland by the former Mrs Miller and her current paramour.'

Vanessa let out a protesting whisper. Her lawyer raised his hand. 'We object to that slur, Your Honour. The gentleman concerned has every intention of marrying my client and, as I hope I have made clear, of treating Abigail as his own daughter in a settled, congenial atmosphere.'

'I think I must sustain that objection, Mr Taylor.'

Taylor bowed his head in friendly acceptance of the rebuke. 'Your Honour. But I am sure you will still see the undesirability of taking a small child away from her own father and her own country to live elsewhere under conditions which, whatever the present assurances, are by no means yet established as lastingly satisfactory or contributory to that child's future welfare.' A note of calculated gravity throbbed in his voice, heading for a final cadence. 'Is there anything else, we would ask Your Honour, any evidence or affidavit you would wish me to add in support of a case which we believe to be legally and morally unassailable?'

The judge added a jotting to the pad in front of him and sat back. He looked with friendly dispassion at Vanessa and then at John Miller, seeming to offer both of them his encouragement.

'I think you've stated the case very well indeed, Mr Taylor.'

Taylor flashed Miller a quick glance. It suggested that they were home and dry: or was it simply that this was how Miller wanted to interpret it?

Leaving the hearing and crossing the Strand with Colonel Railton, Miller said: 'And how bloody long will it take him to deliver judgment? He could have done it on the spot. The whole thing couldn't have been made much clearer.'

'There was some question between the three of them of a minor conflict of jurisdiction between Britain and Eire. Didn't you cotton on to that bit?'

'Meant nothing to me.'

'Don't know that it meant much anyway. But I'm sure the judge was on our side. It's only a matter of reviewing all the factors and then issuing his verdict.'

They stopped on the kerb. On the far side, waiting to come over the zebra crossing, was Vanessa. A man beside her had taken her arm, turned her face towards his, and she was laughing now – a very different Vanessa from the taut, strained woman in that room. Miller took a step forward, his right fist clenching. Railton caught his elbow to hold him back.

And what else would that slimy bastard be touching, tonight and every other night? Even half an hour from now, if they were in a hot hurry, maybe they had a place nearby, a place where they could calm her poor ravaged nerves?

Railton was saying: 'Don't, John. Don't ruin it now. I think ... I'm sure it's going to be all right.'

Mackie was waiting impatiently for him at the Yard, with Collis standing wretchedly, unacknowledged, to one side.

'About time, too. DACC and a chorus of top brass waiting to get going. This way.'

'What's it about, guv?'

'No idea.'

Mackie bustled them along the corridor, through the Deputy Assistant Commissioner Crime's anteroom, and into the office. A number of unfamiliar faces and one or two vaguely known ones, encountered in previous crossings of paths and intentions, appraised them but showed neither approval nor disapproval.

'No lengthy introductions,' said the DACC. 'Miller and Collis, you may know some of Drug Squad.' He waved towards a group keeping themselves very much to themselves in one corner. 'And' – waving grandiloquently again, trying to incorporate a selection of mutually suspicious officers into one big happy family – 'HM Customs, C11, C12, A3. Between us we've all been interested in a number of men. Overlapping in some weird way. Especially one small one, and one big one. The smaller one has a fascinating disc on his car windscreen.'

'The Astra,' said Miller.

'The Astra,' the DACC confirmed.

One of the Customs group said: 'Several of our people have Astras, but from those pictures we know it's a senior man called Rodney Cavan. Senior but not what we think of as sensitive. Unblemished record. Thoroughly vetted, thoroughly reliable in our books. He would have been off duty when those pictures were taken. Perfectly free to visit friends or acquaintances wherever he chose.'

'Friends like that little lot?' queried Collis.

'We're keeping an eye on Cavan.'

'Just as we decided to do,' said the DACC smoothly, 'as from confirmation of identification. Until now.'

Until now . . .? Miller did not care for the sound of that.

'Some of you,' the DACC was holding forth, again

embracing the other branches, 'may not know our CID phrase, "yachtsman". Ronnie Knight type villains have villas in Spain. The bright ones don't have big villas, they have large yachts – in small harbours. The local police come to make enquiries. If they can't be bought off, half an hour later the yacht puts to sea. Our yachtsman, we've established, is one George Edward Payne. Millionaire, but he's been very quiet about the way he got that way. If he's not a bank robber, he's certainly a well-heeled bank exploiter. We're beginning to think there must be every devious deal known to man in his history, except serious "form". Run-of-the-mill blunders, way back. At the moment he's based in the London Embassy Hotel, Hammersmith. As far as we know he doesn't know we know that. For the last few days a large number of those present have been receiving regular memos on the progress of these two here.' He nodded towards Miller and Collis.

The others continued their silent appraisal, as if probing expertly for some indication of criminal tendencies.

The DACC addressed the two of them directly. 'You must have wondered what was going on these last few days, with us allowing you to freelance around what was clearly a major enquiry, basically the province of Drug Squad and Customs. Well?'

'I think we only took instructions,' said Miller cautiously.

'No. You took some highly personal initiatives which we carefully monitored. They worked okay. Did you realize you were being surveillanced by Drug Squad and Customs more or less all the time? Except last night. Unhappily you were not followed up in time to the killings at Bridgetown House.'

'We called for reinforcements.'

'You did. As I've said, it was an unhappy situation.'

Collis said resentfully: 'We didn't know we were being surveillanced. Or that there was any reason why we should be.'

'You did well. Somebody had to plant a bug in Payne's

hotel suite, and all the rest of it. You've contributed. Nobody's used or abused you. You've been a great help and nobody's going to deny that. Now events have overtaken all of us and we must put this investigation on a correct footing. From now on this enquiry will be the exclusive province of Customs and Drug Squad. No doubt over the course of the next few days they'll want to have discussions with you. I'm saying to you two, and to Mr Haldane and Mr Mackie, thanks for the efforts so far. Now it's over to Customs and the Drug Squad. *You* may take no further initiative on this case.'

It was over. They were politely dismissed. On the way back they were silent with disbelief until they reached the door of Haldane's office. Then Miller swung round upon DI Mackie.

'Did you know we were being surveillanced?'

'I sussed it as a possible.'

'They give us a run, and just as we start getting somewhere they cut off our legs.'

'Correct me if I'm wrong,' said Mackie deflatingly: 'you got nowhere.'

In the doorway of his office, DCI Haldane said: 'So they allowed you to stick your necks out – spearhead something. But it's developed. Really opened up. The heroin, plus three murders. Well, some you lose.'

'*We* didn't lose anything,' said Collis stubbornly.

'It's all for the best. Cost-benefit-wise, anyway.'

'Don't read you, sir.'

'You know how it is these days. We've all got our allocations. Mustn't overspend. We have to operate within our budget, not commit ourselves too deeply. Too big a scene, and we try not to go in unless we really have to. They'll roast us afterwards for going over budget. Now it's all in somebody else's ledger.'

Miller was listening with mounting incredulity. Collis shrugged, somehow seemed to have switched off and lost interest.

Haldane looked at him keenly. 'Something else on your mind?'

'I think you know, sir. I've got that black guy in Westminster Hospital. I've put a squad car down a bit of the scenery. Not much of a future for me without a big result.'

'And this was supposed to be it?'

Collis nodded, mute.

'Put in a completion report. Then Inspector Mackie will rota you fresh duties. D'you have a gun checked out, Miller?'

'Yes, sir.'

'Check it in.' As they were about to leave, disconsolate, Haldane said: 'All right, you may think we've been treated badly. Let the clod-footed squad crash about, and if we bugger it up then laugh at us. If we get results, then take it away from us. I know how you feel. But we do exactly what we're told. And you two – let's have no more freelancing. That way lies absolute disaster. Understood?'

'Sir.'

They left, aware that Haldane was watching their backs and that he was probably going to reinforce his warnings to DI Mackie.

It was over. Haldane had said so. And orders were orders.

Two women detectives sat in their Ford Escort below the serried windows of Rendlesham House. WDS Richards was finishing a cigarette as a Sierra pulled in behind them. Miller and Collis got out, Collis bestowing a rueful look on the immaculate paintwork of the Sierra, so unlike another model he knew of.

Richards wound down her window. 'Haven't you heard?'

'What?'

'On Squad net. We're closed out on this. All down to

Customs and the Drug boys. Just having a last drag before pulling out.'

'Yeah,' said Collis. 'That's the ticket.' He waited for Richards to drop her fag end out of the window, and trod on it. 'Look, when you get back to Mackie, don't mention us turning up here.'

The girl's face was grim. 'Freelancing?'

'Could be. Might be. Tell us about target.'

'If we've been ordered to back off –'

'Then you back off like a good girl. But just for the record, tell us. Wrap it all up neatly.'

Richards looked at him without favour, but after a glance at her companion she summed up. 'Mr Cavan got out of bed at seven-fifteen. We assume he had breakfast. Put on his smart uniform, reported to HM Customs, Cargo Terminal Four, London Heathrow. Was there one hour forty-six minutes, then got into his Astra and came here, HM Customs, Rendlesham House, where I believe they specialize in excise duty, tax on the beer to you.'

Ignoring her snide inflection, Collis said: 'I don't see it. Beer tax and George Payne?'

'So in addition to wrecking cars and mugging defenceless black villains, you're now operating a force within the Force?'

'Thanks for your sympathy. Why don't you just sort of wander off?'

'Viv?' Richards looked at her colleague.

WDS Hunter nodded.

'We shall do that,' said Richards coldly.

Miller and Collis watched the Escort drive off. Its departure left a clear view of a telephone box on the corner of the street.

'Before anything else,' said Miller, 'I want to talk to my father-in-law.'

Collis gave him a melancholy, understanding grin, and got back into the Sierra.

John Miller dialled, and waited. There was no pain in

his chest this time; not yet; instead, just a silly fluttering in his breath.

'Railton.'

Miller pressed the money into the slot. His voice cracked. 'Hear anything yet?'

'Oh, John, it's you. I phoned counsel. He's out to lunch.'

'Long bloody lunch hours some people have.'

'I'll keep phoning.'

'You'll leave any message at Squad Office?'

'Yes. Oh, and John ... I do think it went well. And I think Vanessa will be all right in the long run. I've just talked to her. She's here – dropped in to play with Abigail for half an hour.'

'On her own?'

'Yes, on her own.'

Then be damn good and sure she doesn't wander off with Abigail, Miller wanted to shout into the mouthpiece. But he kept silent until Railton went on: 'One odd thing, though. Didn't like to mention it earlier. No point in worrying you at the time when there's probably nothing to worry about. Maybe,' Railton floundered, 'it's not a good idea to mention it now. . . .'

'Out with it,' said Miller.

'Just that when I had a brief word with Taylor, you remember, just before we left ... he said he hoped your job wouldn't count against us.'

'My job?'

'Long hours. Absence from seeing Abigail. He said in real terms it's me and a nanny, as against the child's mother, bringing her up.'

'Vanessa's bloke tried that line. It sounded stupid then and it sounds stupid now.'

'Anyhow, he was still pretty confident. No way the judge will let the child leave the country.'

Miller became aware of Collis signalling frantically from the car. 'Michael, I have to go.'

145

'I'll phone you as soon as I can.'

Miller replaced the phone and hurried across the pavement to the Sierra.

'There he goes,' said Collis.

Cavan had come out of the Customs building and was getting into his Astra. As he moved away, the Sierra settled into the pursuit.

'How was the phone call?' asked Collis.

'So so.'

'Heard anything?'

'Not yet.'

'But it's going to be okay?' Collis was doing his best to sound reassuring.

'It had better be.' Miller hauled his attention back to the job ahead. 'You think we're doing the right thing, both of us sticking on Cavan?'

'You're the intellectual. Me, I just have this gut feeling this is the guy.'

'Right,' said Miller pensively.

He thought of Abigail, and at the same time was thinking of Payne and Khalid Khan and the thread running through it all – drugs. Thought of Abigail growing up, and being trapped before she reached her teens. That was the way it was, these days. He had seen kids hooked early, hooked so early that they never stood a chance of growing to maturity. He knew what it was like and what had to be done. There was no way, having got this far, he wanted to hand over to any other squad.

12 It was not so much a summons to the Government Chief Whip's office as a friendly, hospitable hint that Anthony Webb might care to drop in and have a social chat. However casual the form of the invitation might be, Webb sensed that it was not one to be ignored, or indeed for his response to be long deferred. He presented himself as soon as he could decently leave the sub-committee meeting which had occupied most of the morning.

'Ah, Tony. Do sit down.'

'Roger. Nothing catastrophic, I trust?'

'Far from it.' Roger Denison smiled judicially, his deep voice suffused with the assurance of his own power. 'Off to surgery this coming weekend, I imagine?'

'Got to keep the voters happy.'

'Stella's well?'

'Blooming.'

'Splendid.' These preliminaries courteously out of the way, the Chief Whip said: 'I think I should tell you that we've got a troublesome little Private Member's Bill coming up shortly.'

No such bill, thought Webb, could be really troublesome if the Whips decided not to allow it to be so. There were dozens of ways of killing off any minor irritations of that kind. Perhaps it would be tactless to say that out loud, though: democratic illusions had to be preserved.

'The Member for Scarsdale,' Denison continued, 'has drawn the lucky straw.'

'Oh, *him*. What's he on about this time?'

'He wants to reform the Register of Interests. Says it is not strong enough. Not comprehensive enough. He wants to enforce the declaration of family interests as well as Members' individual interests.'

147

'But we've never allowed the net to be spread that wide before.'

'No, but this Labour crank thinks Members might be in the habit of declaring their own interests freely and frankly' – the Chief Whip's expression was remote and dispassionate – 'while doing all sorts of things on behalf of wives and families which they are not obliged to register. Our friend wants to add this obligation.'

'What's started all this?'

'As I've said, he's a bit of a crank. Not married, of course.'

'Oh. I see. You mean you've got information that he's . . . well . . .'

'Certainly not,' said Denison with righteous dignity. 'That would in any case be none of our concern, unless some security aspects were involved.'

'And family interests are none of his concern,' said Webb. 'Is there any indication that he's got it in for someone?'

'Not necessarily any particular person. We think he's a genuine way-out idealist.' Denison's nose twitched with distaste. 'But there are indications that he has a special thing against Betty Mackenzie. From his point of view she might well be set up as a prime example of a – how shall I put it? – a declaration dodger.'

'Mrs Mackenzie's harmless enough, surely? Only opens her mouth about once every three or four months. I've often wondered if she makes up for it at home.'

'I doubt it. Not with a husband that powerful. Big noise in merchant banking, with some complicated deals in Saudi Arabia. You deal with the Saudis, and you're soon taught that women should be subservient.'

'So what's dicey about Mrs Mackenzie?'

'Clean as clean. On the Register of Interests she quite honestly has nothing to declare: her only interest outside the House is, in all good faith, her own house and being Mr Mackenzie's supportive wife. But how supportive? The inference that some spiteful little ... ah ... bachelor might want other people to draw is that in Parliament and on Parliamentary committees she could be secretly advancing her husband's pecuniary interests without it ever needing to be formally recorded.'

'Do you think she is?'

'No. She's too dim. But you can see where such arguments might lead, or be made to lead. If we let the bill be talked out, as we usually do with such nuisances, and it looks as if things have been manipulated to that end, there's bound to be a lot of bad publicity. Lots of idiots will believe that the deplorable man is on to something dirty which genuinely needs cleaning up.'

'But it'd be ridiculous to let such a motion go through. It's not so long ago that we got over that pathetic enquiry into parliamentary lobbying. The Select Committee on Members' Interest disposed of that one. How many more nigglers do we have to cope with?'

'I had an idea that you might be opposed to it,' said Denison mysteriously. 'But we all have to be sure we have clean noses when it comes up for debate.'

Anthony Webb stared at that bland, domineering face. He did not grasp the implication, if in fact there was one there to be grasped. Surely he had not been brought here to be sounded out either on his views of this cockeyed bill or his personal involvement in ... well, in what? Doubts bubbled to the surface and were hastily thrust down to drown.

In a suddenly brisk, man-to-man tone, Denison said: 'Now, let's get down to it. Today I'm really wearing my Patronage Secretary's hat. I'm commanded to make a discreet approach and sound you out before your name is submitted to the Main Honours Committee.'

Webb's heart gave a wild leap. 'The ... Honours Committee?'

'It has been mooted that the suggestion be put to the PM,' said Denison in his best circumlocutory style, 'that a recommendation should go forward to Her Majesty regarding a knighthood for yourself.'

'A knighthood? Roger, I never expected –'

'Come off it, Tony. You know perfectly well you've been expecting it. It's just that you couldn't be sure of the timing.'

Webb gulped. 'If such an honour is offered –'

'It will be offered, providing circumstances prove satisfactory.'

'Circumstances?'

'There's just this one thing.' The affability was still there, but with a steely underpinning. 'With this awkward business coming up about declaration of interests, and hints about family fiddles, we have to be very careful not to provide the Opposition with free ammunition.'

'I gave up both my directorships when I became a Member. That's on record.'

'There was nevertheless' – Denison picked his way delicately through a moral minefield – 'a matter of that planning enquiry five years ago . . . or was it six . . .?' He let the question hang in the air. He knew perfectly well how many years it had been. 'A bit of a rush, some misguided people thought. One or two so-called experts are still unhappy about the result.'

'This is ridiculous,' Webb let fly. 'The media did their bloody-minded best to stir it up, as usual. But they had nothing to go on – because there *was* nothing to go on.'

'I'm delighted to hear it,' said the Chief Whip, with the suspicion of a lash at the end of his tongue. And then he said: 'What sort of contact do you still maintain with a developer called George Payne?'

Tony Webb went cold. 'Payne? I don't remember. I mean,' he fumbled, 'I didn't deal with anyone called that. Not at the enquiry or –'

'You met him outside the House this very week, and went off with him.'

'I didn't know I was being spied on.'

'You really ought not to get so prickly, Tony. Nobody is spying on you. It's just that people notice this, and notice that, and put things together –'

'And get it wrong.'

'I do agree with you. Like our friend with his obsession about declaration of interests, and switching responsibility to the family, and all that rubbish.' He looked up at the ceiling as if appealing for celestial advice. 'That holiday you and Stella had in Portugal, just after the enquiry. . . .'

'What about it?'

'Who paid for it?' asked Denison dreamily.

'What the hell are you implying?'

'I'm not implying anything. Just to make everything smooth and uncomplicated, I'm *asking*. Your word'll be good enough for me.'

'I paid for it, of course,' said Webb sullenly.

'I was sure you did.' Denison's gaze returned from the unresponsive ceiling. 'You've got receipts for the hotel and the rest of it?'

'Receipts?' Webb's voice was shrill, out of control in spite of all he tried to do to throttle it down. 'You don't keep receipts for a holiday. Not for that long, for goodness' sake.'

'True. But if any snooper wanting to stir up trouble were to visit the hotel and dig through the records, and ask questions round the resort, would there be anything which might embarrass you?'

Webb shook his head, not in denial but in stupefaction.

Denison said: 'Tony, I've told you about the probable recommendation. And I've told you the sensitive area we're in. I implore you to go home and think over any financial interests you or Stella may have, anything you may have overlooked . . . and then come and have another word with me.'

Tony Webb's first impulse was to ring Stella and announce that she was shortly to be Lady Webb. His second, more practical impulse was to ring Mr Hanrahan at the London Embassy Hotel.

Monroe answered the phone. 'Mr Payne's busy.'

'It's very important. I have to speak to him.'

'Can't imagine anything important right now. I thought we'd got everything nicely sewn up. Thanks for your help, and goodbye.'

'Just a minute. That won't do.'

'Won't it?'

'I've got to speak to George.'

'If Mr Payne needs you,' said Monroe dismissively, 'he'll get in touch. Right now he has a lot of important things on his mind.'

'I'm telling you –'

'Don't call us,' said Monroe. 'We'll call you.'

Hanley was looking well content. He had been given a lot to do these last few days, and it was the kind of thing he enjoyed doing. While he still had the appetite for it, Payne thought it would do no harm to keep feeding him opportunities. You didn't win battles by letting the troops sit back and relax. Building up the real killer instinct was a matter of keeping up the pace of the killing, getting them to need the taste of it: keep up the pressure until the real win-or-lose assault was launched. . . .

Hanley was fighting fit right now. It was essential to keep him that way. And Colin Ettrick was down on his knees. It was not merely a matter of keeping him there: more one of making sure that he never recovered the strength to get up again.

No breathing space for either Hanley or Ettrick.

'Try Stakos.' Payne plucked the name from a capacious memory. 'He owes us a couple.'

All the major deals were tidily in hand. Finishing touches were being put to the converted DAF, making it into a tank rather than a goods vehicle. Arrangements on the property front were going smoothly. Payne decided to give himself a breather and indulge himself by accompanying Hanley and Monroe while they did a bit of groundwork.

The two of them were carbon copies of himself: very pale carbons, but at least he could decipher the characters and knew how to interpret them.

The Mercedes arrived outside the London Cyprus Wine Company in Camden Town. Its proprietor, piling wine cases inside the entrance, looked up invitingly at the prospect of customers but lost some of his bonhomie when he saw Hanley and Monroe propped against the door jambs.

'Stakos.' Hanley made it sound a dirty word rather than a greeting.

'A long time.' Stakos would clearly not have minded it being a lot longer.

'Still in business?'

'Always in business.'

'Provided you behave yourself, eh?' Hanley let the words sink in as he stooped over a few loose bottles on top of the tower of cases. 'What's your best plonk?'

'We do not serve plonk. Our best wine is a good bottling of Enotria.'

'Give us a tasting.'

'Thirty-one pounds fifty a case. Then you can taste all twelve bottles.'

Hanley spotted a corkscrew on a nearby shelf and helped himself to it, along with a couple of dusty glasses. Fastidiously he wiped the glasses with a crumpled handkerchief.

'I don't think I've ever risked any Cyprus plonk before. And you, Mr Monroe?'

Monroe shook his head, looking doubtfully from the bottle to the handkerchief which Hanley was stuffing back into his pocket.

As Hanley lifted a bottle towards the light, Stakos said: 'That will be three pounds to you.'

'Before I drink it, there's nothing I ought to know? They do use modern methods of manufacture? I mean, they didn't take off their shoes and socks to grind the grapes? It's not full of mother-in-law's toenail clippings and athlete's foot?'

153

'You don't want to drink it, you don't have to drink it. And now,' said Stakos flatly, 'what do you want? Someone has sent you to talk to me.'

'Ten out of ten.'

'Who?'

'Mr George Payne.'

Stakos looked less scornful. 'He's back in town? Been away a long time.'

'You think so?'

'Interesting. I hear things, over the years. But never anything definite. Except perhaps they always say how rich he is. But England's not a place to spend money, so why come back here? Look at Paris – beautiful shops, magnificent restaurants. He wants to come back to England? He gets soft in the head, yes?'

'Not so it shows.'

'England is crappy.'

'It's full of Cypriots,' said Hanley.

'So Mr Payne is back.' Stakos tried to peer past them towards the Mercedes. Monroe's shoulder was in the way. 'Always an interesting man, your Mr Payne,' said Stakos tentatively.

'You could say that.' Hanley gulped at the wine and made an exaggerated grimace. 'One of his great interests at the moment is Colin Ettrick, you know?'

'Really.'

'Yes, really.' Hanley stared into his glass. 'A little heavy on the anti-freeze.'

'Mr Payne is clever,' said Stakos, 'but Mr Ettrick has a lot of people.'

Monroe spoke for the first time. 'Not as many as he started out with, Mr Stakos. We're doing our best to re-dress the imbalance.'

The two of them looked down on him. Stakos put out a hand on top of the uppermost crate to steady himself. 'What d'you want with me?'

'See much of Colin Ettrick?'

'I . . . oh, I do a little work for him. When it pays. When it suits me.'

'I bet it's not a lot to do with dodgy wines,' said Hanley. 'You'd have to get up very early in the morning to sell Col a bunch of this.' He set his glass down. 'Now listen. And listen good. There's a lot of your boys working on building sites round here, and down Holborn. The ones who don't fawn enough to get jobs as waiters. Used to handling explosives, right?'

'You can't expect me to ask those sort of men to go along with you and –'

'It's not them who'll be going along with us. It's you.'

Stakos's dark forehead was bleached into nothingness. 'Is not my line. I run a wine business now, I have nothing to do with –'

'You run it,' Hanley cut in, 'because a couple of rivals got their premises burnt out. Right? And another one lost an arm and a leg.'

'Literally,' said Monroe with an intent smile, 'or financially?'

'Both. You do remember, Stakos?'

Stakos all too obviously remembered but chose to say nothing.

'So,' Hanley continued with relish, 'you do know a lot about removing unwanted competition. No one would accuse you of having any moral objections against the idea. And that makes you just the man for us. You know Ettrick, and you know the way to remove him. Mr Payne will be very grateful.'

'I can't do this sort of thing.'

'You can't do anything else. Right. Just you get a couple of your chums organized – fast – and over a takeaway moussaka you sort out some deal with them. It shouldn't take much. Nobody will ever notice it's gone.'

Stakos thought of a couple more arguments. It took him about half a minute to propound them, and Hanley ten seconds to demolish them. He and Monroe left with a comradely wave and went back to the Mercedes.

'Fixed?' asked Payne from the back seat.

'Fifty K, twenty-five up front, cash.'

'Your friends come expensive.' Payne brooded over it for a moment. 'You'd better be right about him.'

'I'm sticking my neck out,' said Hanley.

'If you're wrong, I'll cut it off. You'd better stay close to him all the way.'

'I figured that.'

'He makes one wrong move, shoot him.'

Hanley showed no reluctance. He was confident. It was all going according to plan, every last little bit of it.

Hanley sat in Stakos's brown Cortina, calculating the speed with which it could be hidden, resprayed and provided with new numberplates if things went wrong. If they went right, the questions would not arise. At the same time he was watching Stakos on the building site to which he had been escorted. Two fellow Cypriots talked earnestly, nodded and then shook their heads, gesticulated with their arms; and then all turned and looked in the direction of the car. Hanley's trigger finger began to itch.

At last Stakos went inside the builders' hut near the entrance. When he came out he was carrying a loosely wrapped brown paper parcel. Hanley watched the parcel coming closer, watched Stakos lay it gingerly on the back seat and then slide into the driver's seat beside him.

'Got what you wanted?'

'It's not what I wanted, Mr Hanley, you know that. It's what *you* wanted.'

'Watch your rotten manners.'

'You're not hiring me because I got nice manners.' Stakos slammed the Cortina into gear and drove off.

Hanley asked: 'What do you do after the event?'

'I walk away. You think I hang around to make conversation?'

156

'What happens if there are people who see you – and recognize you?'

'They will see me. Everyone will see what a lucky escape I have. And wonder who's had it in for me.' He slowed the car. 'We're near enough. You get out here.'

'Oh, no. Drive on a bit. I want a good view of the garage.'

Stakos reached the corner and stopped. From here there was a good viewpoint on Colin Ettrick's large garage and workshop, respectable cover for a lot of none too respectable things going on behind. A gleam of white within the open doors of the body shop reminded Hanley happily of Johnny Ettrick's injured Porsche. It was going to take some time to straighten out those dents, if anybody bothered with such things, after what was going to happen here right now.

Hanley got out and leaned against the wall, looking distantly up the road while he gave Stakos time to drive on to the forecourt. Then, casually, he turned to watch.

Stakos had stopped just inside the service bay area. He got out, waved a greeting at a man in the car showroom, and got a friendly wave back. As a mechanic poked his head out from under the upraised bonnet of a Jaguar, Stakos gave a more imperious wave.

'Mr Ettrick. Tell him Stakos is here. He's expecting me.'

The mechanic wiped his hands on a rag and went to the wall phone. Stakos peered indifferently into the showroom window, scratching his chin as if not impressed with what he saw. Reflected in the glass he saw what Hanley, from his vantage point, could also make out: Colin Ettrick coming down a few steps at the side, beginning to walk round.

Stakos called out to a forecourt operator serving at one of the pumps. 'You got a bog round here?'

The man pointed to the side of the building nearest him, well away from Ettrick's direction. Stakos hurried into the toilet. Hanley watched Ettrick head for the Cortina and then glance impatiently about him when he found nobody in it or near it.

'Stakos? Where the hell did he –'

The Cortina erupted in a great gout of flame and smoke and flying, lethal shards of glass and metal. A cloud swirled over the whole area. Somebody within it was yelling blue bloody murder; but it wasn't Ettrick. When the smoke cleared, Hanley could see that there was virtually nothing left of the Cortina – and nothing recognizable of Colin Ettrick.

George Payne ticked Ettrick's name off his mental list, and waited for Monroe to report back on the next item. Time was running short. Everything had to be slotted into exactly its right place now. George Payne wanted it all neat and foolproof. His days of clumsy thick-ear stuff had finished long ago. He didn't just put his head down and charge, not any more. Nowadays it was all calculated, and all messy fragments had to be dealt with and swept out of the way – like the fragments of the Cortina and Ettrick.

Monroe was waiting in the underground car park as before. And, as before, Cavan was on time.

The Astra stopped beside Monroe.

'Stay in the motor, Rodney.' Monroe indicated with his thumb a dark shadow standing well along the row of parked cars. 'His name's Hudson. Just like in "Upstairs, Downstairs" – snap your fingers and he brings you something on a tray.' He snapped his fingers.

Hudson got into the van and drove it out of its parking space. Madeleine Cavan was handcuffed to the passenger door again. She jolted to a halt as the van stopped ten yards from the Astra. Cavan tried to get out, but Monroe was leaning on the door.

Cavan's wife was crying without making a sound. She was putting on a wonderful act on their behalf, thought

158

Monroe appreciatively, without any rehearsal whatsoever. He said: 'I hope you've got the right photos this time.'

Cavan held out a large envelope and began to splutter an appeal. Monroe waved him down as he took out the pictures and slanted them to catch the light. They were very good: just what was needed as final confirmation.

'You'll let her go now?' Cavan begged. 'We won't do anything, I promise you. I wouldn't go to the police, not now.'

'Looks like we can take you up on your suggestion,' said Monroe affably, 'that it's possible to make it work earlier. Maybe even today. We could be going in this afternoon.'

Cavan stared at him. 'All right,' he whispered.

Monroe bent closer, enjoying the way the little runt cowered back in his seat. 'You're absolutely positive there's nothing different about the schedules and transfers today?'

'I told you that already.'

'All right. This afternoon, just phone us and confirm that a delivery's on its way. And then make sure you're not around.'

Cavan flapped his hand despairingly in the direction of his wife. 'You're going to let her come with me now?'

'She'll be released right after the job. Pronto. *If* you've fed us the right gen. Now off.'

Cavan, sickened, reversed the Astra and swung back towards the ramp and the exit. Monroe watched him go, pitiless but with a tic beginning in his left cheek.

This afternoon: could they really be ready for the off by this afternoon?

13 John Miller and Jim Collis had been waiting, alert, adding supposition to supposition and still getting blurrily nowhere. But waiting.

They had followed Cavan, still not knowing what the hell was going on and what his involvement could possibly be. They waited for him outside the underground car park without daring to venture too close and find out why he had gone in there in the first place. It was just as well that they had learned patience; learned to adjust to the boredom of the job, the six days of dull routine which might on the seventh day explode into something meaningful.

As they were settling down for a session of wondering where Cavan might walk from here, or where he was next going to drive from here, the Astra roared up the ramp and back out into the street.

Miller flicked the engine of the Sierra into life. He was about to give pursuit when Collis said: 'Hey – watch it!'

A grey Mercedes was emerging from the ramp, signalling to turn left. Cavan's Astra had gone right. Miller caught a glimpse of a profile inside the Mercedes, and braked. 'One of our old friends from the hotel.' He watched the two cars accelerating in opposite directions. 'Which one?'

'Stick with the Astra.'

'I don't know. I . . . oh, hell,' snarled Miller, 'all right. But why?'

Collis had probably chosen right. There had been this continuing contact between that little Customs man and the big-time mob. But still the question was: why?

He settled into formation three cars behind the Astra, forced the pace, and crept up to within one intervening car. That was safe enough; though the little creep was probably not expecting to be followed – too creepy to know what was really going on, Miller assessed from a distance.

But that didn't figure. He was involved, he must know *something*. And what *was* going on?

Prickles rose on the back of his neck. He was sure they were closing in on something: not just on the violence that Payne and his lot had been spraying around as if murder and mayhem would be out of fashion tomorrow, but huddling close to the real motivation behind it all. Close, and still not knowing what was going on.

They were on the City Road now, and the Astra was indicating for a left turn. Miller slowed and pulled out, deceptively signalling to turn right, and then did a last-minute swerve down Maltby Street. Ahead of them the Astra was tipping over a small hill and starting to run down the other side.

Miller reached the crown of the slope. The Astra was signalling again, this time turning right towards the gates of a low, sprawling building set behind high fencing reminiscent of a concentration camp. It went in. Miller drove past at a funeral pace, while he and Collis read off the notice beside the gatehouse.

And it began to make sense.

They were looking at the closely guarded entrance to the Queen's Warehouse Number Two.

It had been here since the days when smuggled or improperly imported goods came in up the river Thames, and confiscated material was housed reasonably close to the dockside. Nowadays the traffic was largely through Heathrow, but the Number Two warehouse, refurbished and heavily protected, was used as an overflow and a special security area to back up Heathrow storage.

Incredible it might seem. Raving mad. But the glimmering was becoming a glow: intuitively they knew just what job Payne and his team were about to pull.

'Central four-four, report location, over.' Miller and Collis stared at the R/T. 'Central four-four, report my signals. State location.' They sat very still. 'Nothing heard. MP out.'

The two sergeants looked back, marvelling, at the Customs building. They had cracked it. In there were nineteen million quids' worth of heroin which seven people had tried to smuggle through Heathrow. Payne and his partners had betrayed them. All heroin confiscated at Heathrow was transferred as swiftly as possible to this Queen's Warehouse: in fact, all heroin, cocaine and grass seized anywhere in England ended up here as evidence, awaiting the trials of the smugglers. Payne was greedy. He wanted not only the rake-off from the stuff his hapless stooges had brought in, but everything else that was in that building – all for himself. As well as the nineteen millions' worth of heroin there could be upwards of twenty, thirty, fifty million quid in cannabis and cocaine.

'Payne and partners are going to raid this dump and steal it all,' said Collis, awe-struck. 'To reveal this information tells Haldane we deliberately disobeyed orders. What do we do?'

'If we tell Haldane,' Miller agreed, 'we'll be under lock and key. If we don't tell him . . . we're free to investigate further.'

'But if we blow it then, having withheld information from the bosses –'

'Then we're well and truly screwed.'

'So?'

'So we head back for the London Embassy,' Miller decided. 'That minor Customs official – he's not the key mover, couldn't be. So let's hope Payne is still at the hotel and we can pick up things from there.'

He started the car, flung it round in a tight U-turn, and accelerated away.

The hotel frontage offered no welcome revelations. There was no way of telling whether Payne, Monroe and any others were inside or whether they had already left and were cranking up their operation elsewhere.

'Watch it!' Collis warned. 'A Drug Squad face.'

162

A taxi parked across the road with its sign unlit held two apparently unhurrying passengers. Obviously the Drug boys had moved in to set up their own surveillance.

'Think his name's Balfe,' Collis added, turning his head away as they drove past the taxi.

Miller turned at a leisurely pace down the side of the hotel, his eyes peeled for other watchers.

'They're not covering the rear,' he announced.

'Lunatics!'

They came to a halt, with a prospect along the side of the building and truncated, unsatisfactory angles on the rear garage entrance and the road at the front. A man could come in or out of the foyer without them knowing. One of them would have to stroll round to the front and keep a wary eye on both the building and the taxi. It might be too late. For all they knew, the whole thing might be getting into gear this very minute, starting from somewhere else entirely.

'Remember how quickly he gathered the team for Bridgetown House,' said Collis apprehensively.

'Right. Once they get going, this lot, they sure do get going.'

'You think maybe we ought to . . .' Collis stopped, stiffened. 'Hey, wasn't that their motor?'

The grey Mercedes slowed past the taxi and came to a halt in front of the hotel. They had to risk it, Drug Squad or no Drug Squad. Miller reversed up to the junction, and they saw Payne getting out of the Merc. The car at once drew away again.

It was the familiar problem: to stay with Payne, or follow Monroe?

Finishing touches had been made to the DAF truck. Extra struts had been welded on to strengthen the ram at the front, and Denton was checking a shortlist of details for the tenth time. It had to be foolproof. Not that any of them were fools: they would not have been working for George Payne if they were.

Payne nodded approval as he passed and went upstairs to the warehouse office. The door of the adjoining toilet was open. Mrs Cavan's eyes implored him over the gag round her mouth. She tried to move and get some message across to him; but her legs and arms were firmly secured.

Monroe had fastened blow-ups of Cavan's dozen photos to the wall with drawing pins. Payne dragged a stool close enough for him to be able to take them all in, panning his gaze slowly along the row. He had reached the end and was starting again as Monroe came into the office behind him.

'Cavan just called from inside the building.'

'I thought he was told to get clear before –'

'He had to sign off. Go through the usual bull. Just a last-minute call to confirm. So . . . it's go. Right?'

Payne nodded thoughtfully. He was concentrating on one picture in the middle of the orderly sequence.

'We're happy that's a photograph of what we're calling Corridor C?'

'Quite sure, yes.'

'I think that's everything, then.'

'Yes,' said Monroe hoarsely.

'Let's get them all together.'

Monroe picked up the phone.

When he and Payne went down by the back staircase, the sight of the gang standing around the completed truck was like a tableau of a platoon ready to go into battle. Crash helmets, face coverings and baseball bats had been piled up alongside two canvas holdalls. Hanley was expertly assembling a sawn-off shotgun. Finch began putting gas grenades into the pockets of a set of army camouflage jackets.

They looked round expectantly at Payne. He set himself in the middle of the yard and looked at his watch.

'One hour and twenty-nine minutes,' he said. 'Now listen, because there won't be time to repeat everything ten

164

times over.' He looked across the yard to the corner of the warehouse which shielded the gateway. Out there was where it was all going to happen. 'We move from here in eight minutes. The sweep through town is timed at forty-five minutes. As arranged, each of you is paired off with one partner from the others we pick up along the way. And you have fifteen minutes to brief that partner. Caution with names, understood? No names. Just numbers, the way we issued them.'

Finch held up one of the combat jackets to show the number stencilled on it.

'We've been over everything many times,' Payne went on, 'but this is the last time. And there's one home truth I think you should know. Get it into your head that this job can't go wrong.' He hammered each word home: 'It . . . can't . . . go wrong. *Mustn't* go wrong. Get that? It's the biggest there ever was. Every detail has been planned to cover all options. But if something totally unforeseen does come up. . . .'

There was a stir of unease.

'I'm only talking about a very unlikely *if*,' snapped Payne. 'And only for your own sakes. If one of you gets hit, or grabbed – do I have to say this? – your families or your near ones will be looked after.' He looked commandingly into each face, then snapped his fingers. 'Right, let's pick up the assistants.'

They moved into place just as they had rehearsed. When Payne was quite sure that every instruction had been observed and every man was where he ought to be, he slid into the Mercedes. Monroe got into the driver's seat beside him. Monroe's knuckles were white on the wheel as he drove out into the street and headed for Hammersmith.

'Well,' he breathed, 'this is it.'

'Right. Last pause for thought. There are two elements which won't tolerate any margin of error. They have to work.'

'Only two?' said Monroe shakily.

'The ramp. It takes the strain or it fails. There's no middle area.'

'A bit late to think about that.' Monroe was edgy. 'But right, there's no middle area. It'll *work*. Guaranteed one hundred per cent. I never doubted it, or Denton's ability to design it.'

'Number Two. Lighting. You're going to take out all the lights. All right, I know, those were my orders, but . . . where you end up, no residual light.'

'George, we've planned all this, we've gone over it a hundred times. You've got to trust the boys from now on.'

'If the mobile lights fail –'

'Torches,' said Monroe tersely.

'A torch in somebody's hand means he's only got one hand free. Torches slow things down.'

'Our lights won't fail.'

They had reached the front of the London Embassy Hotel when Payne said offhandedly: 'Time to tell you something else.'

Monroe sighed. 'What's that?' He waited for another last-minute worry.

'I won't be on the spot,' said Payne.

'Just a minute. I thought –'

'I'll be at a vantage point. I'll see more or less everything. Can you handle it?'

'I didn't expect this.'

'I trust I read you right, David.' Payne was still casual and silky. 'You came into this for a bit of excitement as well as the money. So you're a lucky man. The excitement goes up by a factor of, let's say, fifty per cent.'

Monroe gazed unseeingly in his mirror at a Sierra backing out from the street beside the hotel. 'I'm trying to think whether it makes a material difference, you not being there. Frankly, you're a bit late in the day.'

'But you're working on it. I can see it ticking over. And you've realized I've been planning my presence to be optional all along. Well?'

'Well what?'

'Take it or leave it.'

Monroe looked squarely at him. 'I'll take it.'

Payne got out of the car and headed into the hotel. Monroe drove off. If he felt a brief flash of suspicion about that Sierra, it was soon gone: the car was parked, making no attempt to follow him.

Ten minutes after Monroe had left, George Payne came across the lobby towards the cashier's desk.

'My bill, please.'

'Yes, Mr Hanrahan.'

The bill was put on the ledge before him. Payne signed the American Express slip and pushed it back.

'I trust you had an enjoyable stay, sir.'

'Most agreeable,' said Payne amiably.

'Can we bring your car to the front, sir?'

'No, that's all right.' He put the card and receipt in his wallet and picked up his one small piece of airline baggage.

'I hope we see you again soon, sir.'

Payne headed for the rear of the lobby and made his way through the rear exit to the service access area and the small Mercedes 190E which he had organized for himself – for once not leaving some minion to fix it for him. He got in and sat there for a few minutes, checking his watch against the quartz clock in the fascia and visualizing, in his mind's eye, the progress of that destructive convoy across the city to its destination.

Collis and Miller had watched Monroe's departure, wrestled with their doubts, and made no move to follow.

'We stay with Payne?' said Collis.

It could be the wrong decision. It could be that Monroe was off to set things in motion on Payne's instructions, while Payne himself simply sat here waiting for a report. By then it might be too late to do anything.

Miller edged back into the side street just as the taxi

moved away – to follow Monroe, or in answer to some summons.

From this street they could see the service access. And all at once they could see George Payne walking towards a small Mercedes, getting in, and simply sitting there for a while.

Again Miller felt uneasy: Payne just sitting there, and all the real action was happening somewhere else.

Just as he was about to voice his uncertainty, an MP voice sounded in the car. 'Central four-four. Report signal and state location. Urgent. Report signal and state location.' They both shook their heads slightly. 'Also message for DS Collis. Phone Westminster Hospital, registrar's office.' There was an attentive pause, then: 'Nothing heard. MP out.'

'Registrar?' said Collis. 'Not intensive care?'

'What does that mean?'

'It means something's happened to the black guy,' said Collis wretchedly.

'You want to phone?'

'If it's bad news, it's too late.' Collis braced himself. 'I'll wait. We've got to get a result here.'

Sunlight glinted on something within the Mercedes. Payne had lifted his car phone. A moment after he had replaced it, the car moved off, emerging round the back of the hotel, well away from any surveillance the Drug Squad might still be maintaining. Miller, grunting with satisfaction that something was actually in motion at last, kept in comfortable range, easing his way into the traffic behind Payne.

It was difficult to guess at Payne's destination. He was not heading directly for the Queen's Warehouse but weaving a complicated route of his own, obviously knowing every short cut and back double on his old familiar territory. The general direction seemed for a while to be that of Pimlico, but there was no telling quite where they would end up.

Miller was almost caught unawares by the Mercedes slowing and pulling in suddenly to the side. He slewed in to a recess by the road and found that it was a bus-stop slot. Nobody was waiting by the sign. He could only hope the service was an infrequent one at this time of day.

So far as they could see, Payne had settled down to another period of meditation. Or waiting. For something, someone: a message, an appearance.

Light gleamed again within the Mercedes. This time it was not the phone but the rear-view mirror tilting to another angle. Payne's head blanked it out as he sat up straighter in his seat.

Miller glanced at his own wing mirror. A small procession of cars was rolling up and passing him at precise intervals, driving very circumspectly. Collis let out a throttled shout. They both saw one of the faces from Bridgetown House; and there was another which had cropped up somewhere in the recent past, somewhere and somebody far from desirable. They all had to be members of Payne's team. It was like a circus on the move.

As they passed the Mercedes, Payne pulled out, fell in behind, and then overtook and began to lead the way.

It was impossible for Miller to give chase past those intervening vehicles. They would be bound to spot that something was up. All he could do was keep a discreet distance behind the convoy.

Over the crown of a hill the group accelerated down a wide roadway. Miller drew closer than he had meant to, and was forcing himself to fall back when he heard Collis curse. Speeding down a filter road to the left was Payne's Mercedes. Miller stamped on the brakes. It was too late and too blatant to swing back and pursue Payne. Anyway, the convoy was what seemed to be carrying the weight and the sheer menace.

'We can't use the radio,' he growled. 'Bet your sweet life they're listening on every available frequency, just in case.'

'Screw the whole thing,' Collis agreed. 'A team moving,

and suddenly panic in Customs and Drug Squad. So it's watch your language, eh?'

'We need three mobiles, well laid back. Look' – Miller drew in at the kerb and was reaching for the door handle – 'I've got to get a cab, get to the Yard, talk to Haldane face to face.'

'You're serious?'

Miller waved Collis towards the driver's seat. 'Don't lose them. Or the motor. Steer clear of steep embankments, right?'

As he sprinted away, Collis was saying into the R/T: 'Central four-four. Instruct DCI Haldane that Miller's coming in. Requires urgent interview with DCI Haldane. Very important . . . and personal.'

'Central four-four, report signal and state location. Urgent. State location.'

Miller waved wildly at a taxi, bundled into it, and re-hearsed what he was going to say when he confronted the DCI. He was breathless as he hurried in, to be collared by Mackie and marched into Haldane's office like a soldier on a charge of breaking at least five Queen's Regulations in addition to dumb insolence, conduct prejudicial to . . . and all the rest of it.

Haldane must have been rehearsing, too, in readiness for this showdown. He had contrived to turn himself an unbecoming shade of purple in the face before Miller entered the room at the double.

'*You* –!'

'Sir, I –'

'What sort of conduct is this for a supposedly sober, responsible officer? Has Collis contaminated you? Dis-obeying orders, charging off, racketing about the place like –'

'Sir, it's urgent. Please listen.'

While Haldane gulped for breath to continue his harangue, Miller swiftly summed up what had happened. When he had finished, Haldane remained the same colour

170

and his voice was at the same pitch of outrage. 'The Deputy Assistant Commissioner Crime spoke to you and that idiot companion of yours, spoke to you *personally* and *ordered* you to stay away from a Customs, Drug Squad enquiry. Trespassers will be shot down in flames. It ought to have been clear enough. And now you're telling me there's a team out there, ready to go, and you want *us* only? You know what? That Collis has destroyed your mind. You're mad!'

'Sir –'

'Three years of damned hard work in the Squad. Not a single dot on your copybook, let alone a blot. And now in one afternoon you want to do more damage to yourself, to Squad, than anybody in the bastard history of this place. Sit down there! While I phone Drug Squad and Customs.'

'Sir!' It was ferocious enough to halt Haldane's right hand on its way to the phone. 'Don't you see what we've got? And I mean that – what *we've* got, not them. All those seven arrested at Heathrow, that didn't make any sense. Only nineteen million pounds of heroin, plus a bonus of grass and cocaine – that's what makes sense, for the likes of George Payne. A few decoys, a few of somebody else's they've been tipped off about . . . and there's all that stuff stored away nice and ready in one place for them. All they have to do is concentrate on that one place. Saves an awful lot of swanning around.'

Haldane's features were still flushed, but his tone was tinged with the beginnings of comprehension. 'And just where is this one mighty haul in one place?'

'Where do all the confiscated drugs go, pending those bunglers' trials?'

'Number Two Queen's Warehouse,' said Haldane softly.

'Payne is all lined up to knock off that Number Two.'

'He's mad.'

'He's mad to get his hands on it, to get in there and shift it and start selling it all over this country. And if you think how mad his methods have been these last few days –'

'Nineteen million quids' worth.' Haldane whistled through his teeth. 'And Christ knows how much cocaine and cannabis already stashed up in there. All right, Miller.' He reached for the phone, and this time Miller did not try to stop him. 'I can get two of our mobiles out right this minute. Put CID on standby. But we'll have to get more support than that. From the sound of it, we need the bloody SAS.'

He looked up from the phone. Miller was heading for the door.

'You come back. Back here, sit down!' But Miller was starting to run along the corridor. 'Godalmighty . . .!'

Miller pounded down the stairs from the fourth floor and out across the Yard's underground car park. In the Robbery Squad sector was a Ford Granada. That would do very nicely. He had the driver's door open and was throwing himself in when the security officer spotted him.

'Hey, you. Wait! That's not your mobile.'

The Granada gathered speed, tyres squealing on the turn up the ramp, and out on to the street.

Mackie, as irate on the R/T as Haldane himself could have wished, was haranguing Collis. 'Is this clear, sonny – you don't make one move. You just stick to their tail till Customs and Drug Squad get themselves mobilized. Then it's over and out, so far as you're concerned. Until then, don't lose those people.'

Just keep the kettle on the boil until someone's ready to make the tea: that was what it amounted to.

Then it was John Miller's turn. 'DS Miller. Location?'

'Hendridge Road, heading east.'

'Two mobiles en route.'

'Hold them west of me.'

'Central, DI Collis on watch. Switch to channel 9.'

Miller leaned forward to switch channels. 'Jim, where are you? And I do mean *where?*'

'Tidal Basin Road. Close to you know where. White BMW, Mercedes, black Granada. Parked.'

'Wait for me.'

'Message understood,' said Collis. Which did not necessarily mean that he intended to obey it, if something else caught his fancy. Miller put his foot down.

On open channel WDS Richards' voice came in, with an excited husky throb that made her sound almost sexy. Miller was not interested – in that department there were thoughts that had to be shoved right to the back of his mind right now – but maybe Collis was getting the message. Knowing Collis. . . .

'Suggest location,' Richards was urging.

'Proceed Queen's Warehouse Number Two, off Tidal Basin Road, lower end. And wait.'

'Message received.'

The cars were converging on the site. But so were Payne's vehicles. Some of them must by now be settled in place. And Payne's men were ahead, knowing exactly what they were supposed to do.

While Miller still did not really, in his guts, believe it. The theories were right, he was sure of that, and knew Haldane was convinced now. Still, in the light of ordinary day, it was incredible.

The late afternoon traffic was beginning to build up. Amazing how many men could afford to knock off work that early. It took not just skilful driving but downright rallying to carve out a route through the tangle. And it was no use using sirens which could be heard a mile away – or closer than that, where you least wanted them to be heard.

Miller forced his way into the last, long street with the security gates right down there at the far end. An angry fusillade of horns and screeching brakes showered him from both sides. To his left, as he cut across the swathe of impatient traffic, he saw the Sierra tucked away out of the main congestion. He spun the wheel, ignored a few more choice fanfares on horns, and slung the Granada to within a few inches of the Sierra's rear bumper.

Both he and the stationary Collis were passed by a slowly accelerating Mercedes. They both stared, checked; did not need to get out and confer; pulled out and headed on past the gates of the Queen's Warehouse, with Payne in his Mercedes leading the way and then, once again, dodging off down a side turning.

It was impossible to tell whether he knew they were on his tail: impossible to guess whether he was leading them unknowingly towards the climax or knowingly luring them away from it.

14 Three vehicles sat silently positioned beside the arches of the railway track parallel with Tidal Basin Road. The line-up consisted of a BMW, a Granada, and a Mercedes. Another car sat separately, unseen by the occupants of the compact group of three: a Sierra, parked by Collis in the cover of a large trailer.

Something else remained unobserved by Monroe and the other drivers in the team: Payne's Mercedes 190E which had crept along between the arches beyond the railway line. After a quiet recce it settled itself into the shadow of one of the arches.

Collis poised himself half in, half out of his car to keep an eye on the motionless convoy. They showed no flicker of activity, but they were not simply filling in time. Something had to happen. And soon.

Hanley got out of the Granada and rested one hand on the door, peering along the road towards the hunched hill over a canal at the end.

Something was on its way.

The noise of an approaching vehicle, invisible beyond the hump of the bridge, started to rise inexorably until echoes jangled under the arches. Collis quit the car to take a wary squint around the end of his sheltering trailer, in time to see a huge truck heaving into view: an armoured nightmare of a converted DAF coming monstrously on as if to start a whole new war singlehanded.

It was a signal for action. Hanley ducked back into his car and started the engine. The DAF slid in behind the convoy and waited obediently like a trained, lumpish circus animal with more weight than brains. At the same time Monroe was nudging the grey Mercedes forward to park by a phone box on the pavement. Collis could see him go

175

into the kiosk and dial. He was taking his time, waiting, keeping the whole street in view.

Now another vehicle was making its entrance. It was less ferocious than the DAF, but armoured securely enough in its own way. It was a ten-ton lorry with the lettering of HM Customs & Excise along the sides.

Monroe dashed back to his Merc. The convoy moved off slowly at his signal, careful not to attract the attention of the Customs lorry driver.

Collis gave them time to disappear under the arches and then pulled out. He knew by now which route they must inevitably be taking, and was able to catch up with them by a quick diversion round three back streets. He emerged not a hundred yards away from Queen's Warehouse Number Two. The Customs lorry was slowing as it approached the gatehouse. The predatory convoy had split up into separate units, drifting with no apparent lack of connection to park at varying distances from the warehouse entrance.

Collis barked into the R/T: 'DS Collis to Miller. Large DAF truck – bloody tank, if you ask me – and three support vehicles, all shifted towards our prime site. Now stationary in new position Laidlaw Street.'

'Acknowledge new position,' Miller responded. 'I know where you mean. Wait for me.'

'Where are you?'

'Couple of minutes from you. Stay put. *Repeat:* stay put and wait till I get there.'

Two men had jumped down from the DAF and slid a grill up over the windscreen. Inside, the driver was putting on a crash helmet.

Hanley in the Granada looked round for a last-minute check that Ennis and Finch were properly equipped, ready to go with the baseball bats in their hands.

The security guard at the warehouse gate was chatting to the driver of the lorry. Neither of them was in any mad hurry. It was routine, it happened regularly enough for

176

them to have ceased worrying. The gates hung open; the lorry began to roll without haste into the yard.

Abruptly the DAF truck roared into action. Veering across the road, it pulled round to charge head on at the closing gates. One security guard, his mouth gasping open, made a wild attempt to swing one of the steel gates shut, but nothing would have stopped the juggernaut now. He jumped for his life as it rammed its way through, smashing the gate to one side and roaring on its course towards the inner warehouse. Three cars followed instantly, in well-timed succession. Security guards who rushed forward were clubbed back with baseball bats.

'Miller, it's started!' Collis raged into the R/T. 'Like we said. The warehouse. Smashing through the gates, a team out attacking the guards. Bloody commando stuff. I'm going in.'

'You've no chance. Not on your own. One minute and I'll be there. You got it? Move one inch and I'm finished with you. Hear me?'

Collis forced himself to stay put. But he wasn't going to make it last for long. Through the swinging gate and the mesh of the fence he saw an iron bar rise and fall. Glass sprayed, somebody yelled, and stopped yelling. A Customs man was being dragged out of the lorry, out of Collis's line of sight. The poor sod didn't even have a wrench to defend himself against that flailing iron bar.

The BMW, DAF and Merc braked to a halt on the forecourt. One man ran back to heave the gates shut and drop the steel locking bars into position. The gates quivered and thrummed once as the Granada was backed into them, blocking them from the inside. Alarms were beginning to set up a raucous clamour over the walls and rooftops. Security men stumbled out of the warehouse, then dived for cover as a spray of bullets rattled around them and three men came on at them with baseball bats.

The DAF thundered into position, backing up to the main doors of the warehouse unloading bay. Three men threw open the truck's rear flaps with the unfaltering accuracy bred of repeated rehearsal. They secured chains from the ramp inside to the loading bay edge of the building. In the driving seat, Denton accelerated forward a fraction. The chains dragged the ramp out of the rear of the truck. The other three, cursing and blinding, dodged and then plunged in again to get a grip, manhandling the ramp up against the concrete lip foundation of the building.

The DAF backed away and started revving again, the huge diesel wailing up from a feral snarl to screaming pitch.

In the Sierra, Collis too began pumping up the revs on his vehicle. He knew that any second now he was doomed to do something insane, but the hell with it, who could sit here and do damn-all while all that was going on in there?

Miller's car slithered to a halt beside him. Collis waved him wildly towards the closed gates. The alarms went on howling above their heads, eventually drowned by the infernal screech of the DAF.

Inside those gates, the truck was describing a half circle round the yard to build up power and speed. Then it levelled up and went straight at the warehouse. At fifty miles an hour its wheels hit the ramp. It knifed up and over the concrete lip, steamrollered through the outer wall of the building showering bricks around it like confetti, and rampaged on through an office, pulping a partition, and on through another curtain wall.

Customs men ducked, scattered, and tried to regroup. They were trained, but not for this runaway nightmare. The practised team beat them savagely aside and drove them away, deeper into the building.

'This way!' Monroe shouted.

Hanley and Finch were running through the ripped line of walls to reach Denton in the truck, but Monroe, with a photographic memory of the plans and photographs in his head, waved them peremptorily down a side corridor from the main hall. Two Customs men tried to brave them. Hanley let off two barrels. One man went down, the other reeled away. Hanley let him go. First things first.

Monroe had reached the security cage, walled in by wire mesh. He blew open the lock on the door with his shotgun. Another alarm was triggered off, but added little to the general discord. The three men burst in and set about methodically lifting the plastic bags of heroin from their neat rows on the bulging shelves, each carrying a couple of armfuls at a time back to the BMW. Monroe carried his quota and then started the engine, staying in the car while the other two went back to complete the haul.

He looked at the dashboard clock. So far everything had gone exactly according to schedule.

The two mobiles arrived at the gates. Miller and Collis sprang out, and Collis began clawing his way up the left-hand gate. He was on the verge of swinging himself over the top when somebody inside spotted him and let out a yell. A shotgun spewed, bullets screeched off the edge of the gate.

'Down, you flaming idiot!'

Miller leapt up and dragged Collis off the gate to one side. As another burst of firing rattled about them, he returned the fire with his revolver.

Through the interstices of the security fence there was another, more vicious blast from within. The two sergeants backed away and crouched for cover round the backs of their vehicles. Collis offered up a silent prayer that the Sierra didn't take too much of a beating: he had been blamed more than enough for damage to models of this kind already.

It was too damned frustrating to be pinned down here like this. Desperately he looked back over his shoulder. Where the hell were reinforcements? The whole district ought to be swarming with relief forces by now.

An empty Green Line bus was coasting unconcernedly

down the road. If the driver considered there was anything odd about two men crouching behind cars or
about the pandemonium raging over the other side of the
fence, he showed no sign of wanting to stop and investigate.

Collis shot up to his feet and planted himself in front of
the bus, flagging it down. The driver blared his horn, came
on, then skidded to a halt and leaned out ready to start an
argument. Collis flashed his ID and, without waiting to
answer any of the spluttered protests, reached in and
hauled the man out bodily into the street, leaping up to
take his place. Ignoring the last wail of indignation he put
his foot down and accelerated straight across the road into
the gates. The impact nearly shook him from the wheel,
but he held grimly on as the gates shuddered and twisted
inwards, curled over the Granada that had been backed
against them.

There was no way the DAF was going to find its way
out over that warped barricade.

All at once the road was busy with traffic. Two mobiles
scudded down from the eastern end, another Sierra came
racing up from the west and screeched to a halt. WDS
Richards was driving. Two men in the back got out fast.
Richards grabbed the handset.

'Central eight-niner, central eight-niner.'

'Come in central eight-nine.'

'On location Queen's Warehouse Number Two. Sitrep,
four police mobiles present. I see five armed men –
probably more inside the building – clubs and firearms.
With support vehicles inside the compounds. Request
urgent reinforcements and ambulance.'

Four policemen scrambled through gaps in the barrier.
Inside, Hanley and Denton were tottering across the yard
to the BMW, their arms piled high with plastic bags. As
a police marksman fired two warning shots, three Customs men took advantage of the distraction to leap out
of hiding and intercept the heroin collectors. A baseball

180

bat fended one of them off. Another skidded and fell heavily.

The BMW revved up and charged the third. As he pushed himself away from the bonnet and crashed over a pile of scattered bricks from the demolished wall, the car slewed round and headed for the gates. The Granada had been tilted to one side by the impact of the bus and the gates, leaving just enough space for anyone crazy enough to risk driving over one edge of the left-hand gate and hoping to straighten up under the side of the bus.

There was no other way out. Monroe chanced it. Stripping shreds of paint off, scouring a panel and losing his offside mirror, he bashed his way through and skidded wildly out on to the road. Collis grabbed a chunk of wood which had dropped off or been torn off something in the upheaval, and crashed it through the windscreen of the BMW as it careered along, half on the pavement and half off. Monroe narrowly missed an oncoming car, skated along the gutter, and tore away.

Collis and Miller ran for Miller's Granada.

'Round the corner – block him off!'

Miller did not need Collis's frantic exhortations in his ear. He raced along Tidal Basin Road as Monroe veered under one of the dark arches. It couldn't have been better. The man was losing his nerve or couldn't see well enough through the remains of his windscreen: Miller knew that the little lane under the arch led nowhere but back out again, three more arches along. He slowed, waiting for the BMW to re-emerge. As it reeled out he jolted to a halt, and was out of the Granada with his gun ready. One single shot did it. The BMW lurched erratically on its way for a few yards, then swung violently and ploughed its way into the side of the arch. The driver's door was sprung open. Monroe fell out, tried to keep his balance, and then groped helplessly towards the murky brickwork before collapsing to the ground.

'That Merc over there!' Collis was calling jubilantly. 'Our

friend who led us all the way to this little circus! Let's go get the ringmaster.'

'It's the one from the hotel. Payne's.'

They clambered past the wrecked BMW, up and over a footbridge, and down to the 190E standing on the far side of the track.

Miller held his gun two-handed in front of him. With Collis tense behind him, ready to spring, he stopped a few feet from the car.

'George Edward Payne. Get out of the car.'

There was no response. Warily Collis edged round the far side. Miller reached swiftly for the handle of the driver's door.

The car was empty.

The atmosphere in Haldane's office was markedly more cordial than it had been of late, even though the DCI was trying as a matter of disciplinary principle to act detached and offhand.

Instead of plunging straight into an official postmortem he spared a minute for Collis. 'Call logged about forty minutes ago. Westminster Hospital. The black gentleman you beat into a coma has apparently come out of it. He's off the danger list.'

The misery of it had dragged on for so long that Jim Collis was not really ready for the news that at last it was over. He could not take it in. He looked, and felt, more shattered than relieved.

'Well, now. Back to today's little operation. It looks like we might have a prospect for a talker. Roy Ennis – hauled him out in pretty battered shape – told us Mrs Cavan was in a warehouse lift. Anyhow, a good result.'

Miller tried to raise a smile from Collis. Good result, good news all round.

'Enough of a result,' said Haldane drily, 'that I don't think we're going to have too much of a problem with Customs or the Drug Squad. Even that lot aren't utterly incapable of showing some gratitude. In spite of. . . .'

182

He left it ominously in the air. Letting us off, thought Miller with a gush of relief: but not too lightly. Watch your step from now on, boy, was the message.

He said: 'Thanks, sir.'

'As for you' – Haldane, having been momentarily benevolent towards Collis, made it clear that his tolerance was not to be trusted too far – 'for the moment we won't be throwing you out. For the moment, right?'

'Sir.'

'But any more wild work . . .'

'Yes, sir. I mean no, sir.'

'Right. Get on with it, both of you.'

The two sergeants made their escape. As they approached the Squad office, the noise of voices made it sound like an office Christmas party. Congratulations began erupting the moment they walked in through the door.

'Terrific!'

'Nice work.'

DI Mackie gave Miller's left arm the faintest punch. 'Nice work,' he echoed dourly. With Mackie, like Haldane, the goodwill wouldn't last more than twenty-four hours, if that. But it was good while it did last.

'John!' The sergeant telephonist on duty was lifting the phone receiver.

Miller's hand fell away from another warm handclasp.

'Your father-in-law. He's phoned a dozen times since two o'clock.'

Miller pushed his way round a desk and a table and seized the receiver.

Railton said: 'John? I'm afraid I've got . . . pretty bad news.'

'Bad?'

'Taylor called. The judge is allowing Vanessa custody, and presumably permission to take Abigail to Ireland.'

Vanessa . . . custody . . . Ireland . . .? It had never really, deep down in his mind, been a possibility. Not really. Couldn't be.

'You there, John?'

'Yes,' said Miller hoarsely. 'Yes, I'm here.'

Across the office, through the surge of jokey congratulations and somebody slapping Collis repeatedly on the back, he caught Collis' stricken, understanding gaze.

'I can't understand it,' said Railton. 'Nor can Taylor. I just don't know what to say.'

Miller had no idea what to say, either. He tried not to look at Collis, because Collis wanted to convey something to him but wasn't going to put it into words either, because there weren't any words.

'Look, Michael,' said Miller at last, 'I'll get back to you shortly. As soon as I can. I'm in the middle of something now. I'll . . . we'll talk later.'

The babble in the room went on, generous but unheeding. 'Terrific result . . . smack in the eye for some of our bossy chums, eh? . . . did it in the end . . . a nice one . . . one hell of a result. . . .'

Too true. One hell of a result.

15 Mrs Payne's displeasure surfaced within less than half an hour of her son's return to the yacht, looking forward to a spell of warm tranquillity after his rather noisy time in London.

'How could you do it, George? I just don't know how you could be so thoughtless.'

He had already picked up some of the English papers on his way through Paris, and there had been lurid stories in a number of international papers on sale in his hotel there. Names were not yet being named, but enquiries were proceeding, and there were one or two disturbing references to a handful of captured criminals and to men who were helping the police with their enquiries. It was believed, according to one columnist, that some of these enquiries might lead to coastal resorts in Spain or Portugal.

An airmail edition of the *Daily Telegraph* and a copy of the local news sheet were lying on the settee in the yacht's main salon as he poured himself his first drink and prepared to relax. But his mother was not prepared to let him rest right now.

'It's not as if I'm as young as I was, George. How could you be so heartless?'

She could hardly have failed to see the headlines and the news stories, and might have been putting two and two together while he was on his way back; but it was the first time he had known her raise any queries about his work or hint at any criticism.

'What have I done this time, then?' he asked.

'That dreadful Florrie Hall. How you could go away and leave me on my own with that awful woman, week after week. . . .'

'Ma, you were the one who begged me to fix for her to come here and keep you company.'

'Not for all *that* time. And don't call me *ma*.'

'No, mother.'

For another twenty minutes she subjected him to a harrowing account of Florrie Hall's misdemeanours, her dreadful conversation, and her drinking habits. Such a coarse person, Florrie Hall. It was that background of hers, of course: a whole family of petty thieves and con-men. What could you expect?

George Payne nodded at appropriate intervals and made sympathetic or disapproving noises where necessary. When the tirade abated he summoned Alvaro, who respectfully poured Mrs Payne a large port and brandy.

The following day Payne's attention was attracted by a motor launch apparently pottering about in the bay but managing to make several inquisitive circles of the yacht while doing so. Lots of tourists took day trips out with the fishing boats or tours in launches like this, and respectful notice was usually drawn to some of the luxury craft in the marina or riding out at anchor. But the faces in the boat did not look like those of holiday-makers.

They looked even less like it when Payne spotted them in the Avenida da Liberdade late that afternoon. These two men were not sightseeing, not contentedly drinking in the sunshine, and not spending their holiday money in a wild carefree way. They looked glum and restricted: men on a fixed allowance, every escudo of which would have to be accounted for when they got back to wherever they had come from.

He called Barata in to a secluded bar a long, healthy distance from police headquarters.

Antonio Barata confirmed his suspicions. 'There are two men asking a lot of questions. They check dates, that sort of thing, you know?'

Payne could guess.

'My friend in the Guarda Nacional, he tell me your name is spoken,' Barata went on. 'I think it is not healthy for you here. Not for some time.'

'Your people don't go much on extradition procedures, do they?'

Barata's palms turned philosophically upwards. 'May be, may not be. Portugal is England's oldest ally. It may be friendly gesture. And if not, there may be help in a . . . shall we call it kidnapping?'

'Whisked away in handcuffs?'

'It has been done.'

'Well' – it was Payne's turn to be philosophical – 'I suppose I'll have to resign myself to moving along the coast for a while until this blows over. Back to Spain for a rest cure.'

Barata shook his head. 'Is different in Spain these days. Not very good at extradition agreements before, but now there is the EEC and they want to be very good boys. There is Gibraltar. And there will be extradition treaties and a lot of co-operation, to show that the old days are over.'

'You're a cheerful sod, aren't you?'

Antonio Barata said: 'I think you go into the Mediterranean. Across to the other side.'

'You do, do you?'

'I buy you out.'

'You do what?'

'We have worked well together, Mr Payne. I represent you nicely, yes? I learn a lot. Now I buy you out, and you represent *me* – in Tangier, yes?'

'What the hell has Tangier got to do with it.'

'We continue the drug traffic. That is easy through Tangier. I trust you, you trust me.'

'Don't bank on it.'

'And there are other interests. I shall be happy for you to expand those. And you can finance them out of our deals together.'

'What other lines did you have in mind?'

Barata smiled benignly. Obviously he had been giving the matter serious thought. Reluctantly Payne realized that he was going to have to make some kind of deal. Less reluctantly, he admitted that he preferred working with someone who had done just that: given the matter serious thought.

'I think we should talk at length in Tangier,' said Barata. 'You ask me, Mr Payne, I think it is time you slipped anchor.'

George Payne was beginning to think the same. By daylight next day the cruising launch, if it came out for another recce, would find an unoccupied parking slot out in the bay.

He was not keen on being bought out, but even less keen on being arrested or otherwise abducted because of continuing too stubbornly on his previous way. Tangier it had to be, for the time being at any rate.

Mrs Payne was indignant. 'They're all *different*,' she protested. 'Not like us at all. I mean . . . they're so dirty. And you can't trust them. I like to be with white people I can trust.'

George Payne refrained from pursuing this argument. Instead he said: 'We'll stay aboard most of the time, the way we always do.'

'That awful food –'

'I don't know who the supplier of the best hotels is,' Payne promised, 'but I'll find out.'

He found out. He also found that Barata had not been mistaken in implying that there were plenty of interests for an entrepreneur like himself. It took very little time to set the existing drugs trade on a more reliable footing. But on top of that there was quite another trade: as a free port, Tangier had retained a devious independence since the halcyon days of its neutral and profitable international zone, and still attracted tourists and resident expatriates with free-ranging tastes. There was quite a lucrative market in women for the visitors, women for import and export. And not just women. Certain quarters in the town were a paradise for English remittance men and a number of Americans with similar desires.

In a few short months George Payne had established himself comfortably. His name was not bandied about in public, but it was known to the men to whom it was important to be known. A new pattern shaped up, not too different from the one he had designed at Albufeira. There was an efficient minimum of work; hours in the pool and a number of relaxing hours ashore; and the leisurely, appreciative scanning of English and Continental newspapers.

Reports from London on the property front were reassuring, though he was not altogether happy with the executives who had been brought into replace Monroe and his henchmen. The business supplements ran a couple of stories about George Payne's enterprises, and hinted as closely as they dared without running risks of libel about his absence from the country and his involvement in less reputable enterprises. There was a lull, a period of retrenchment; but the progress was quietly made.

Also there was an interesting story with which Payne did not at first concern himself, other than in a remote reminiscence. A debate in the House of Commons on Members' privileges and financial interests sparked off some angry exchanges between the Government and the Opposition, and there was talk of one mysterious matter being referred to the Public Accounts Committee. One scurrilous magazine went so far as to run a derisive story on the whole affair alongside an apparently irrelevant story about Mr Anthony Webb's disappointed expectations of a knighthood because of a hinted clash in the Political Honours Scrutiny Committee.

Two weeks later Mr Anthony Webb, MP, resigned and announced that he was returning to his business interests and perhaps diversifying into property development.

'This dreadful food,' Mrs Payne continued to complain. 'I'm sure it's not safe to eat.'

'At least it'll keep your friend Florrie away,' Payne soothed her.

'No friend of mine.'

'It'd bring her out in hot flushes.'

'No need to be coarse, Georgie. If I've told you once, I've told you a hundred times. Really, I can't imagine what sort of people you've been mixing with.'

George Payne applied himself to developing a nice sideline in expensive international time-share complexes. A hostess-cum-housekeeper cost extra. There was a minor problem in finding the right wording for the advertisements, conveying the right message without inviting prosecution. No problem in finding the women themselves.

He was only very mildly surprised when he received a letter from Tony Webb. It had taken a fortnight to reach him by devious routes. Webb did not know his current address, and if Payne chose not to reply there would be no way he could find it. At first he was tempted not to reply, anyway. The plaintive note in Webb's writing style had the same whining tone in it as his voice. And Webb seemed to think that he, George Payne, was under some moral obligation to help him. Webb had grandiose ideas about playing a leading role in Payne's property developments, representing him while he was out of the country, keeping things running smoothly no matter what Payne's own current difficulties.

Payne had little time for drips like Anthony Webb. Use them, drop them: that was how it had always worked so far as he was concerned.

But he found himself toying with the idea. With the right incentive and the right training, Payne saw that Webb could be a useful stop-gap until things could be reorgnized in a big way. Fly him out here, spell out the whole deal to him, make sure he understood the rewards and the possible penalties, and that would be one load off Payne's mind until he was ready to reassume it.

Until. . . .

George Payne realized his own weakness. He had grown bored with the sardines, the squid, the *linguada* and the *gambas*, and the harsh *vinho tinto* of Portugal; and bored

190

with the third-rate, small-time crooks he'd had to deal with if he wished to pass the time in anything more entertaining than swimming, sunbathing or sweating over some girl in a rented apartment. Now, in even shorter time, he was wearying of the couscous and the imported frozen foods and the garish pseudo-European hotels and the smell of the markets and bazaars.

Things had gone wrong in London. The coup hadn't worked. But that didn't mean that some other venture would not work, given time, given the right planning and the right team.

George Payne was getting bored again.